Fatal Corrections

Cozy Quickies

Dalia Bolin

Published by Gettin' Cozy, 2023.

Blurb

When the pen is mightier than the sword, editing can be murder.
IN "FATAL CORRECTIONS," a riveting installment in the Cozy Quickies line, bestselling romance author Clary Lane finds herself at the heart of a murder mystery. When her editor, Brenna Cath, is found murdered with a red pen through her heart at a secluded writers' retreat, Clary's world of romance and happy endings is shattered.

Trapped on the island by a raging storm, Clary finds herself surrounded by a cast of characters straight out of a mystery novel. There's the enigmatic horror author Ethan Scoville, who's caught Clary's eye; Timothy Small, the self-help guru with ample reason to hate Brenna; Martha Masterson, a cookbook author with a past as spicy as her recipes; and Bella Anderson, a young romance author with a flair for the dramatic and burning ambition.

As Clary delves deeper into the mystery, she uncovers a web of secrets, lies, and blackmail. With each revelation, it becomes clear everyone had a reason to want Brenna dead. In a world where the pen is mightier than the sword, Clary must find the killer before the final page turns... and she becomes the next victim.

Chapter One

THE DAY THE INVITATION arrived, Clary Lane was contemplating the merits of becoming a hermit. She was nestled in her favorite armchair, a half-finished manuscript on her laptop, and a cup of lukewarm tea on the table beside her. The mailman's knock on the door was a welcome distraction from the stubborn characters refusing to cooperate in her story.

She shuffled to the door, scooping up her mischievous cat, Mr. Darcy, who had a habit of making a break for it whenever the door was open. "Not today, Darcy," she said, scratching behind his ears as she picked up the stack of mail.

Back in her armchair, she sifted through the pile: Bills, a postcard from a friend traveling in Italy, a flyer for a local pizza place, and a cream-colored envelope with an embossed logo. Clary's mouth got dry. She recognized the logo. It was Brenna Cath's.

Brenna Cath, the editor who could make authors cry with a single red mark on their manuscript. The woman who had a reputation in the publishing world that made Voldemort seem like a misunderstood introvert. And now, she had sent Clary an invitation.

Clary opened the envelope with a sense of foreboding, half expecting it to explode or turn into a bat. Instead, out slid a card with an invitation to a writers' retreat at a private island. Clary snorted. "A retreat with Brenna Cath. Sounds about as relaxing as a root canal."

Mr. Darcy, sensing her agitation, pawed at the invitation. "You want to go, Darcy?" asked Clary, raising an eyebrow at the feline. "Maybe Brenna could edit your meowing at 3 a.m."

Despite her initial reaction, Clary found herself staring at the invitation, her mind a whirl of thoughts. She glanced at Mr. Darcy, who had now curled up on the armrest, seemingly uninterested in the life-altering decision she was about to make. "You're a lot of help," she said, scratching the cat's head.

With a sigh, she reached for her phone and dialed a number she knew by heart. Emily, her younger sister, picked up on the second ring. "Clary? This is a surprise. You usually text."

"I know, Em, but this is a matter of life and death."

Emily's laugh echoed through the phone. "Dramatic as always. What's up?"

Clary explained about the invitation, her voice rising in pitch as she described Brenna Cath. Emily listened in silence, only interrupting with an occasional "uh-huh" or "go on."

When Clary finished, there was a pause. "So, let me get this straight," Emily finally said. "You've been invited to a writers' retreat on a private island by the most feared editor in the publishing world, and you're considering going?"

"Putting it that way makes it sound insane."

"Because it is," said Emily, "But it's also an incredible opportunity. You've been stuck with your writing for months. Maybe this is exactly what you need."

"But it's Brenna Cath, Em. She's...she's..."

"A shark in editor's clothing?" Emily suggested, and Clary could hear the grin in her voice. "Come on. You've faced worse. Remember that time in college when you had to read your poetry in front of that snooty literature professor?"

Clary groaned. "Don't remind me." She wasn't a poet and definitely "knowed" it, especially after Prof. Turney humiliated her.

"Exactly. You survived that. You can survive Brenna Cath."

Clary sighed, looking at the invitation again. "Maybe you're right."

"I usually am," said Emily, her voice filled with sisterly affection. "Now, go pack your bags, Clary Lane. Adventure awaits."

As she hung up the phone, Clary couldn't help smiling. Maybe Emily was right. Maybe this retreat was exactly what she needed. And if not, well, it would certainly make for an interesting chapter in her next book. Too bad she wrote romance instead of horror since Brenna was a horror story.

Clary stared at the invitation, her mind a whirlwind of thoughts and apprehensions. Finally, she let out a sigh, her decision made. "Well, Darcy," she said, glancing at her cat, who was now attempting to eat the corner of the invitation, "It looks like I'm going on an adventure."

She moved to her bedroom, pulling out a suitcase from the depths of her closet. As she began to pack, she reflected on her career. The early days of excitement and late-night writing sessions fueled by cheap coffee and cheaper pizza. The thrill of seeing her name in print for the first time, even if it was in a magazine that had a readership of twelve.

A chuckle escaped her as she folded a sweater. She remembered her first meeting with Brenna Cath. The woman was as warm and cuddly as a cactus and had the uncanny ability to make authors cry by merely raising an eyebrow. Yet she was also the best in the business, and Clary had to admit, she owed a lot of her success to Brenna's ruthless editing.

She paused, holding a pair of jeans and wondering if she should pack a swimsuit. "Who am I kidding?" she said, tossing the jeans into the suitcase. "The only swimming I'll be doing is in a sea of adverbs and misplaced commas."

Her relationship with Brenna was complicated, like trying to solve a Rubik's cube while riding a roller coaster. There was respect, fear, and a constant pressure to meet Brenna's high standards, but there was also gratitude. Brenna had pushed her, challenged her, and in the process, made her a better writer.

With a shake of her head, Clary zipped her suitcase. She had a retreat to attend, and if she was lucky, she might even find the plot for her next novel. "Watch out, Brenna," she said, a smirk playing on her lips, "Here comes Clary Lane."

CLARY STOOD AT THE dock, her suitcase at her feet, and took in the motley crew that were to be her companions for the next week. She couldn't help but feel like she had stepped into a novel, and not one of the romance ones.

First, there was Martha Masterson, the cookbook author. She was a petite woman with a smile that could outshine the sun and a laugh that sounded like wind chimes on a breezy day. Her Southern drawl was charming if as slow as molasses. She was currently engaged in a lively conversation with her handbag, which Clary found both endearing and slightly concerning.

Next was Timothy Small, the self-help guru. He was a nervous little man with a few stubborn hairs clinging tenaciously to his pate as he constantly adjusted his glasses and glanced around as if expecting a pop quiz at any moment. He was clutching his latest book, "Finding Your Inner Zen in a World of Chaos," so tightly that Clary feared for the safety of the book's spine.

Then there was Bella Anderson, the new romance novelist. She was a vision of elegance and grace, her every move seeming like it was choreographed. Tall, blonde, and speaking with a New England accent, she looked like a supermodel or a famous politician's spoiled kid, not an up-and-coming romance author. She was currently engrossed in her phone, her fingers flying over the screen at a speed that would put professional typists to shame.

And finally, there was Ethan Scoville, the horror novelist, who was as hot as his last name. He was tall, dark, and brooding, looking like he had walked straight out of one of his own novels. He was standing a little apart from the group, his gaze focused on the distant horizon.

Clary couldn't help but chuckle. She was about to spend a week on a secluded island with a woman who talked to her handbag, a man who looked like he was perpetually on the verge of a panic attack, a woman who probably had more followers on social media than Clary had words in her latest novel, and a man who looked like he was auditioning for the role of 'mysterious stranger' in a noir film.

"Well, Darcy," she said, though her cat was safely with Auntie Em, as she pulled out her phone to send a quick text to Emily. "This is going to be one hell of a retreat."

She quickly typed out a message, her fingers dancing over the screen. *"Hey, Em, just checking in. How's our furry escape artist doing?"*

As she hit send, she felt a pang of guilt for leaving Mr. Darcy behind, but Emily was a good cat-sitter, even if she did complain about Darcy's 3 a.m. serenades. And besides, Clary had enough on her plate with the upcoming retreat.

As they boarded the boat, the tension was so thick she could cut it with a knife. Or a particularly sharp quill, Clary mused, glancing at her fellow authors. They all looked like they were on their way to the gallows rather than a writers' retreat.

Martha was clutching her handbag like a lifeline, her knuckles white. She was murmuring something under her breath, a recipe perhaps. Clary wondered if it was for a comfort food dish. She could certainly use some comfort food right now.

Timothy was pacing the deck, his book clutched tightly in his hands. He looked like he was reciting something, probably one of his self-help mantras. Clary hoped it was working because he looked about two seconds away from jumping overboard.

Bella, on the other hand, was still engrossed in her phone. Her fingers were flying over the screen, probably tweeting about the retreat.

Clary could just imagine the hashtags—**#WritersRetreat #NervousWreck #TooPrettyForThis.**

And then there was Ethan. He was leaning against the railing, his gaze fixed on the horizon. Clary wondered if he was plotting his next novel or just trying to avoid conversation.

As the boat chugged along, the island looming closer with each passing minute, Clary felt a sense of impending doom. She pulled out her phone to send another text to Emily. *"If I don't make it back, tell Darcy I love him, and he can puke up hairballs into my favorite slippers."*

With a sigh, she hit send then tucked her phone away when her sister didn't immediately respond. Emily was a work, like a responsible nine-to-fiver, so she probably wouldn't text back for a few hours. She just wished for the moral support, since she had a retreat to survive, after all. Maybe it wouldn't be as bad as she feared. Or maybe it would be worse than she imagined, and she had a vivid imagination.

As the boat chugged along, the silence became too much for Clary. She cleared her throat, turning to Martha. "So, Martha, working on any exciting recipes?"

Martha looked up, her eyes wide. "Oh, yes. I've been experimenting with gluten-free pastries. It's quite a challenge, you know."

Clary nodded, her knowledge of gluten-free anything limited to a disastrous attempt at baking cookies. "Sounds interesting."

Timothy, overhearing their conversation, said. "I've been trying to incorporate more gluten-free meals into my diet. It's supposed to be good for reducing stress."

Ethan snorted, not looking away from the horizon. "I doubt any diet can reduce the stress of dealing with Brenna Cath."

Bella looked up from her phone, a smirk playing on her lips. "Perhaps the no-air diet. Death might be the only way to escape."

The conversation lapsed into silence again, but it was a more comfortable silence this time. They were all in the same boat, literally and figuratively, and there was a strange comfort in that.

FATAL CORRECTIONS

Clary leaned back, watching the island grow closer. She had a feeling this retreat was going to be anything but boring. The boat bobbed on the waves, the authors bobbed on a sea of anxiety, and somewhere in the distance, Brenna Cath was probably sharpening her red pens.

"Anyone up for a game of 'I Spy'?" asked Clary, breaking the silence. "I'll start. I spy with my little eye...something beginning with 'D'."

"Dread?" Timothy suggested, his eyes wide behind his glasses.

"Doom?" Ethan added, finally tearing his gaze away from the horizon.

"Doughnuts?" asked Martha hopefully, her hand instinctively reaching for her handbag.

"Drama," said Bella, her eyes back on her phone.

Clary laughed, shaking her head. "Nope, it was dock, but I like your answers better."

As the boat pulled into the dock, Clary shuddered. She was about to embark on a retreat with the most feared editor in the publishing world and a group of authors who could be characters in their own novels. What could possibly go wrong?

Chapter Two

THE BOAT BUMPED AGAINST the dock, the sound echoing in the silence. One by one, the authors disembarked, their faces a mix of anticipation and dread. Clary was the last to step off, her gaze drawn to the imposing house that loomed in the distance.

It was a grand old mansion, its once vibrant colors faded by time and weather. Ivy crawled up the walls, framing the darkened windows like nature's own picture frames. It was the kind of house that would be the perfect setting for one of Ethan's horror novels.

Martha was the first to break the silence. "Well, isn't this... quaint," she said, her voice wavering slightly. She clutched her handbag tighter, as if expecting a ghost to jump out at any moment and make off with her moisturizer.

Timothy was already flipping through his book, his lips moving silently as he read. Clary wondered if he was looking for a chapter on how to survive a spooky mansion.

Bella, on the other hand, was taking pictures, her phone clicking away. Clary could already see the Instagram captions—**#HauntedMansion #WritersRetreat #SendHelp**.

Ethan was staring at the house, a strange smile on his face. "I've always wanted to stay in a haunted house," he said, his voice filled with excitement.

Clary rolled her eyes, a smile tugging at her lips. "Let's hope it's not actually haunted."

With a collective deep breath, they moved toward the house. The front door creaked open, revealing a grand hallway. Dust motes floated in the air, dancing in the slivers of light that filtered through the heavy curtains.

As they explored the house, each room revealed a new piece of history. A grand piano in the drawing room, its keys yellowed with age, a library filled with books, their pages brittle and smelling of time, and a dining room with a long table, set as if expecting guests.

The house was spooky, yes, but it was also fascinating. It was like stepping back in time, each room a snapshot of a bygone era. She could almost hear the laughter and conversations that once filled these rooms.

They dispersed to find their rooms, a game of eerie musical chairs. Clary's room was on the second floor, a cozy space with a four-poster bed and a window overlooking the sea. She was unpacking, her clothes a colorful contrast to the room's faded elegance, when a knock echoed through the room.

"Come in," she said, expecting one of the authors.

Instead, the door creaked open to reveal Brenna Cath. Her silhouette filled the doorway, a dark cloud blotting out the sunlight. The room seemed to shrink in her presence, the air growing colder. She didn't bother with a greeting as she said, her voice as sharp as a scalpel, "I hope you're ready to work."

Clary straightened, her heart pounding. She met Brenna's gaze, a challenge in her eyes. "Always am. You know me."

A smile flickered on Brenna's face, as brief and chilling as a winter's day. "Yes, I do. That's why I invited you."

Clary couldn't help but raise an eyebrow. "And here I thought you invited me because you enjoy my sparkling personality."

Brenna's laugh was dry, a sound that echoed in the room long after it had ended. "Your personality is as sparkling as a three-day-old fish. Fortunately, your characters are livelier." With that, she turned on her heel and left, the door closing behind her with a soft click. The room seemed to breathe a sigh of relief, the tension easing slightly.

Clary let out a sigh. "Darcy," she said to the empty room, "This is going to suck."

She returned to her unpacking, her mind buzzing with thoughts. Brenna Cath was here, and she meant business, but Clary wasn't one to back down from a challenge. She was here to write, and write she would. Even if it meant facing the storm that was Brenna Cath.

She was the first one to make it downstairs for dinner, her stomach growling like a disgruntled bear. The smell of food wafted from the kitchen, a tantalizing aroma that promised more than just the canned soup she was used to.

She was about to make a beeline for the dining room when she noticed Ethan. He was standing by the window, his silhouette framed by the dying light of the day. He looked...contemplative, like a philosopher pondering the meaning of life, or a writer trying to come up with a killer plot twist.

"Trying to figure out if the butler did it?" asked Clary, sidling up next to him.

Ethan turned, a grin tugging at the corners of his mouth. "Just enjoying the view."

Clary followed his gaze, taking in the fiery hues of the sunset. "It's beautiful, like a Bob Ross painting."

Ethan chuckled, the sound blending with the distant crash of waves. "Happy little trees included."

Their shared laughter echoed in the room, a moment of camaraderie, but the moment was fleeting, broken by the sound of footsteps. The rest of the authors were descending, their voices a symphony of anticipation and anxiety.

"I guess it's time to face the music. Or in this case, the dinner."

Ethan nodded, his eyes twinkling with amusement. "After you."

As they headed toward the dining room, Clary felt a strange sense of optimism. They were all in this together, after all, and maybe this retreat wouldn't be as horrifying as a room full of clowns.

The dining room was a grand affair, the long table set with an array of dishes that would make Martha's cookbooks jealous. The authors gathered around, their conversations a low hum in the background. Clary found herself seated between Ethan and Timothy, who was already flipping through his self-help book, probably looking for tips on how to survive a dinner with Brenna Cath.

Brenna, at the head of the table, raised her glass, the chime silencing the room. "I'd like to propose a toast," she said, her voice carrying an edge sharper than the steak knives, "To a productive retreat."

Glasses clinked, the sound echoing in the silence that followed. Brenna continued, her gaze sweeping over the authors. "I hope you all brought your best work. After all, there's always room for improvement. Or there's the option of no room."

The veiled threat hung in the air, a guillotine ready to drop. Clary exchanged a glance with Ethan, his gaze mirroring her unease. The room was filled with tension, the authors suddenly as stiff as the starched tablecloth.

Brenna's smile was as cold as the chilled wine. "Enjoy your dinner."

Bella hadn't put down her phone until that moment. It landed against the table with a *thunk*. "Ugh, why can't I post? Do you know how many Instagram and TikTok followers are waiting for my updates on this du...retreat?"

Brenna's smile widened, a shark circling its prey. "Oh, didn't I mention? There's no internet or phone connection here. Consider it part of the retreat experience."

Bella's mouth dropped open, her eyes wide with horror. "No internet? No phone? But my followers..."

Clary couldn't help a chuckle. "Welcome to the dark ages, Bella."

Brenna raised a hand, silencing Bella's impending rant. "Don't worry. We have a radio for emergencies. Now, let's enjoy our dinner, shall we?"

As the meal resumed, a chill ran down her spine. The retreat had officially begun, and they were more isolated than she'd realized. It was clear Brenna wasn't here to play nice, but then again, neither was Clary. She was here to write, and she would be damned if she let Brenna scare her off.

After all, as the saying went, the pen was mightier than the sword. And Clary was ready for battle.

As the dinner progressed, the conversation flowed like molasses in January. Martha was attempting to discuss her latest gluten-free pastry experiment, her hands kneading an invisible dough in the air. "Gluten-free is the future," she insisted, her eyes wide with enthusiasm that somehow seemed feigned as she glanced nervously at Brenna every few seconds.

Across the table, Timothy nodded, his fingers nervously tapping against his book. "I've heard it's good for reducing stress." It seemed to be his standard reply to Martha's babbling about gluten.

Ethan, his gaze fixed on his plate, grunted. "I'm game if it reduces the stress of dealing with Br...this."

Brenna, at the head of the table, let out a laugh that sounded more like a hyena's cackle. "Ethan, dear, if you're stressed, you should try Timothy's book. I hear it's a real cure for insomnia."

The table fell silent, the authors exchanging uneasy glances. She could feel the tension rising, like a balloon ready to pop.

Just then, the door swung open, revealing a man with a frazzled expression and a stack of papers in his hands. Adrian, Brenna's harried assistant. He gave the authors a small wave before making his way to Brenna's side, whispering something in her ear even as his gaze briefly rested on Bella before quickly moving away as she turned from him. Clearly, she had no time for lowly assistants.

Brenna's smile didn't falter, but her eyes hardened. She turned back to the table, her gaze sweeping over the authors. "Adrian has received your latest chapters and tells me they're all dreadful."

She frowned, feeling that was unfair, especially since Adrian had requested they send them last-minute before departure.

"It seems we all have our work cut out for us this week. Martha, your pastries could use less gluten and more flavor. Timothy, your self-help book could use less jargon and more...help. And Ethan, your horror stories could be a tad less horrifying. Clary...you're the same as ever." She made that sound like a personal failing despite Clary knowing how to tap into what her readers wanted and give it to them in new ways.

Bella seemed on edge, clearly expecting Brenna's scathing remarks too.

Instead, the evil editor looked away from her without a word before addressing the rest of them. "I suggest you all get a good night's sleep. You're going to need it."

After dinner, the authors migrated to the rec room, a space that looked like it had been decorated by someone with a fondness for taxidermy and a lack of restraint. Brenna had excused herself with a curt nod, leaving the authors in a stunned silence. It was like the Wicked Witch had left, and they were the Munchkins, blinking in the sudden sunlight.

Clary found herself drawn to Bella, the new romance novelist. She was sitting alone, her gaze fixed on a stuffed moose head above the fireplace. There was a certain desperation in her eyes, a hunger that Clary recognized all too well.

"Bella, how are you finding the retreat so far?"

Bella turned, her smile a little too bright. "It's...educational. I've never been in a room with so many egos before."

Clary chuckled, remembering her own first retreat. "It can be overwhelming, but it's also a great opportunity to learn and grow."

14

Bella's smile faltered, her gaze dropping to her hands. "I just hope I can keep up. I mean, you're Clary Lane. Your books are...everywhere."

Clary felt a pang of sympathy. "Thank you, but I was once where you are now. We all start somewhere."

Bella looked up, her eyes filled with a fierce determination. "I want to be successful. I want to write books that people love, that make them feel something."

Clary reached out, giving Bella's hand a reassuring squeeze. "And you will. Just keep writing, learning, and most importantly, keep believing in yourself."

Bella's gaze flickered to Clary's hand on hers, a hint of envy in her eyes. "I do, and I didn't come here to make friends. I came here to win."

As she pulled her hand away, Clary felt a chill. The retreat had just begun, and already the claws were coming out.

Clary left Bella to her ambitious musings and moved to join the others. Martha was in the middle of a passionate monologue about the merits of organic farming. "You see," she was saying, her hands shaping an invisible vegetable in the air, "When you grow your own food, you're not just feeding your body. You're feeding your soul."

Timothy, his eyes wide behind his glasses, leaned forward. "That's fascinating. Do you think there's a correlation between the food we eat and our mental well-being?"

Martha nodded enthusiastically. "Absolutely. When we nourish our bodies with wholesome food, it positively impacts our mental health."

He was nodding along. "That's very insightful. I should include a chapter on organic farming in my next book. 'Nourishing the Soul: A Guide to Inner Peace through Organic Farming.'"

Ethan, who had been staring into the fire with the intensity of a man trying to telepathically communicate with it, snorted. "I think I'll stick to my diet of pizza and despair, thanks."

Clary couldn't help but laugh. "Ethan, you're a ray of sunshine, you know that?"

Ethan turned to her, a smirk playing on his lips. "I aim to please, but seriously, I think we can all agree the real key to mental well-being is surviving this retreat with Brenna."

The room filled with laughter, a shared camaraderie in their mutual dread of their editor. As the laughter died down, Clary turned to Timothy. "So, what's your latest self-help book about?"

Timothy adjusted his glasses, a nervous habit Clary had noticed. "It's about finding inner peace through embracing change. I believe that change, though often scary, is a natural part of life that we should learn to accept rather than resist."

Ethan raised an eyebrow. "Sounds like something Brenna should read."

The room erupted in laughter again, with even Timothy chuckling behind his hand. The conversation flowed from there, each author sharing their work, their process, and their struggles. They spoke of late nights and early mornings, of writer's block and sudden inspiration, of the joy of a well-crafted sentence and the frustration of a plot hole.

Martha shared her journey from a home cook to a cookbook author, her eyes shining as she spoke of her love for food. "Food is more than just sustenance," she said. "It's a way of bringing people together, of creating memories."

Ethan, in his typical dry humor, shared his experiences of writing horror. "There's something cathartic about scaring the bejesus out of people," he said, a wicked gleam in his dark eyes.

As the evening wore on, Clary found herself drawn into their stories, their passion for their craft. Despite their different genres, they all shared the same love for storytelling and the same desire to touch people's lives through their words.

As the evening wound down, the authors retired to their respective rooms. The storm that had been brewing all day was now in full swing, the wind howling like a banshee and the sea churning restlessly. Clary stood by her window, watching the storm with a sense of awe and trepidation.

She pulled out her phone, her fingers flying over the screen as she texted Emily even though there was no reception to send the message. *"Day 1: Survived dinner with Brenna. Ethan is a horror novelist with a diet of pizza and despair. Martha is on a mission to make the world gluten-free. Timothy is a bundle of nerves with a self-help book for every situation. Bella is a ticking time bomb of ambition. Wish me luck."*

After a moment, she sent another message. *"In the original haunted mansion cliché, but no ghosts yet. The night is still young though."*

She spent a few more minutes watching the storm, the lightning illuminating the turbulent sea, before deciding to call it a night. As she crawled into the four-poster bed, the wind whistling through the cracks and the house creaking in response, Clary wondered what would happen tomorrow. With one last look at the storm outside, she turned off the lamp and surrendered to sleep.

Chapter Three

THE STORM WAS IN FULL tantrum when Clary awoke, the house groaning under the onslaught of wind and rain. She laid in bed, her heart pounding in sync with the thunder outside. Something felt off, a prickling sense of unease that had nothing to do with the storm.

She got out of bed, wrapping her robe around her against the chill. The house was eerily quiet, the only sound the howling of the wind and the occasional creak of the old wooden floorboards. She moved to the window, watching the storm rage outside. It was in this moment of quiet contemplation that she saw it—a figure lying motionless in the back garden.

Her heart skipped a beat. She squinted, trying to make out the figure through the sheets of rain. It was Brenna. Clary's breath hitched. She was lying face down in the mud, her body eerily still.

She rushed out of her room, her mind racing. She found Ethan in the hallway, his face pale in the dim light. "Ethan," she gasped, her voice barely audible over the storm, "It's Brenna. She's in the garden. She's not moving."

His eyes widened, and he followed her to the nearest hall window to gaze down at the garden. The horror novelist looked genuinely terrified.

"Help!" Clary shouted, her voice echoing through the house. "Something's happened to Brenna."

One by one, the authors emerged from their rooms, their faces reflecting the same fear. As they gathered in the hallway, their eyes darting between each other and the storm outside.

"What is it?" asked Bella with clear irritation as she tied her robe belt.

"Brenna...I think she's dead."

A collective gasp followed Clary's words. The news of Brenna's death hit like a physical blow. Martha let out a gasp, her hand flying to her mouth. Timothy dropped his self-help book, his eyes wide, though he must have forgotten his glasses. Ethan looked like he had just walked into one of his own novels. Bella was the only one who remained eerily calm.

"She can't be," she said firmly. "Brenna Cath couldn't die."

"She looks pretty dead to me," said Clary as she pointed to the window nearest them.

For a moment, they all just stood there crowded around the window, the reality of the situation sinking in. Brenna, the woman they had all feared, hated, and respected in varying degrees, was dead. And they were stuck on an island with her body.

Bella broke the silence. "We need to call the authorities," she said, her voice steady.

Clary nodded, pulling out her phone only to be met with the all-too-familiar 'No Service' notification. She let out a frustrated sigh, the weight of their situation settling on her shoulders. "There's no signal here. Remember?"

They were trapped on an island with a dead body and no way to call for help.

"But Brenna mentioned a radio," said Martha. "We can use it to call for help."

The authors exchanged glances, their faces pale and drawn. The storm outside raged on, mirroring the turmoil inside the house.

Martha frowned. "What are we waiting for? Let's find that radio."

As they moved to action, a chilling thought crossed Clary's mind. They were not only trapped on an island with a dead body, but also with a murderer. And until help arrived, they were all potential victims.

With a newfound sense of urgency, they made their way to Brenna's office, hoping it was the most logical place for the radio to be kept. The room was as imposing as the woman herself, filled with dark furniture that looked little used and the distinct scent of strong coffee. The radio sat on the desk, a relic from another era.

Clary reached for it, her heart pounding in her chest. She turned the knobs, but all she heard was static. A closer inspection revealed the reason—the wires at the back had been cut. "It's sabotaged," she said, her voice barely above a whisper.

The room fell silent, the only sound the howling of the wind outside. The implications were clear—they were not only trapped on the island, but someone didn't want them to leave or call for help.

"We need to check the boat," said, Ethan his voice steady despite the fear in his eyes.

Clary nodded, pulling on her jacket after retrieving it from the coatrack in the hallway. "Let's go then."

As Ethan reached for his own jacket, Clary noticed his hair was wet. "Have you been outside already?" she asked, her eyes narrowing.

Ethan ran a hand through his damp hair. "No, I just showered. I was heading downstairs for a snack when I ran into you. I have trouble sleeping in new places."

Clary nodded, though a small seed of doubt sprouted in her mind. They braved the storm, making their way to the dock. The boat was moored at the dock, bobbing violently in the choppy waters. The boat was there, but a quick inspection revealed the engine had been tampered with. They were truly trapped.

With a shared look of dread, soaked and shivering, Clary and Ethan returned to the house. The others were waiting in the living room, their faces pale in the flickering firelight. Clary couldn't help but think they all looked like characters in one of Ethan's horror novels—trapped in a haunted house with a dead body and no way to call for help. It would have been funny if it wasn't so terrifyingly real.

"The boat's been sabotaged. We're stuck here," said Clary.

The room fell silent, the only sound the crackling of the fire and the storm raging outside. They all looked at each other. They were trapped on an island with a murderer.

Martha sounded on the edge of panic. "This is just like one of your novels, isn't it, Ethan?" she said, her voice shaky. "A group of people trapped in a haunted house with a killer on the loose."

Ethan, who was wringing his wet hair with his hands, looked up. "I usually write supernatural horror, but I wish it were just a novel, Martha."

Timothy, who had been flipping through his self-help book, cleared his throat. "We need to stay calm and rational. Panicking won't help."

Bella, who had been silent until now, spoke up. "Timothy's right. We need to figure out what to do next."

Clary couldn't help but snort. "I don't suppose you have a chapter in your book on what to do when you're trapped on an island with a murderer, Timothy?"

Bella shot her a glare, but Clary just shrugged. If she was going to die on this island, she was going to do it with her odd sense of humor intact.

The silence was broken by the crash of thunder, making them all jump.

"What if she isn't dead?" asked Timothy softly. "She's been out the for a while now. If she's still alive..."

What a grim thought. Why hadn't any of them thought to check that first thing? Still, recalling the odd angle of Brenna's body, she doubted Timothy had any reason to worry about Brenna lying in the rain and catching a chill. She was already ice cold to Clary's way of thinking.

"I guess we should go get the body...check on Brenna." She glanced around at the others, her gaze finally settling on Ethan, who'd just stripped off his jacket. "Want to help me drag a corpse through a raging storm? I know that's like a dream come true for you horror writers."

"She could be alive," said Timothy stiffly.

She nodded without any conviction. "Sure."

Ethan gave her a wry smile. "As tempting as that sounds, I think I'll pass."

Clary rolled her eyes. "Fine. Then I nominate..." Her gaze landed on Timothy, who looked like he was trying to become one with the couch cushions. "Timothy, since you're so concerned she's still alive. Congrats, you've been selected for corpse retrieval duty."

Timothy's eyes went wide behind his glasses. "Me? But I...I don't think..."

Clary grabbed his arm, pulling him to his feet. "No time to think. We have a survivor to save...or a body to collect."

She dragged a stammering Timothy out into the storm, Ethan trailing reluctantly behind them after grabbing his jacket again. The wind whipped at their faces as they made their way to the garden. Brenna's body lay where they had seen it earlier in the same position, her pale skin made even more ghostly by the dark mud covering her.

"Do you want to check on her, Timothy?" She was unsurprised when the nervous man shook his head. With a sigh, she knelt in the squishy mud with a grimace, examining the body. That's when she saw it—a red pen sticking out of Brenna's chest, right through the heart. "It looks like someone took Brenna's editing a little too literally."

Timothy looked like he might gag as Ethan arched a brow. "Someone who understands irony. The murderer must be an author."

Between the three of them, they managed to haul Brenna's body back inside. They laid her on the couch in the currently unused living room, the authors gathering around, shock and fear on their faces.

"All right," she said, turning to the others, "We need to figure out who killed Brenna while we're stuck here. Any suggestions on where to start, mystery gang?"

The wind howled outside, emphasizing their isolation. The game was afoot, and for better or worse, they were the players.

The authors looked at each other blankly. Mystery solving was clearly not their forte.

Finally, Bella said, "Shouldn't we notify Brenna's assistant? He's here somewhere, isn't he?"

Clary snapped her fingers. "Adrian. I completely forgot about him."

Leaving Brenna's body laid out in the living room, they trooped upstairs. Adrian's room was at the end of the hallway. Clary pounded on the door.

"Adrian, we need to talk to you."

He didn't respond.

Bella curled her lip. "He probably stayed up late talking to his wifey and is dead to the world."

"No phones or internet, remember?" asked Ethan.

Clary knocked again, more firmly this time. Still no response. She tried the handle. Unlocked. The door creaked open to reveal a room bathed in early morning light streaming through the windows—and Adrian sprawled face down on the floor.

There were identical gasps behind Clary. Martha clutched her ever-present handbag to her chest.

"Please tell me he's just passed out drunk," said Ethan.

Clary knelt and rolled Adrian over. His face was frozen in a look of terror, and a fountain pen stuck out of his chest.

Clary stood up. "Nope, not drunk. Though he looks pretty calm considering he's been stabbed with a writing implement."

Ethan eyed it for a moment. "It looks like someone stabbed him while he was sleeping. See, he might have just fallen out of bed when he was stabbed."

"I'd imagine that makes sense, because he would have put up a fight otherwise," said Timothy.

"So why was Brenna outside in the rain?" asked Bella, though she didn't really seem to care.

Clary hesitated and then shrugged. "Maybe she was awake and ran from her attacker?"

"If so, she should have called for help," said Martha.

She nodded her agreement, still having no explanation as she turned to the authors who were staring with wide-eyed alarm.

"We've got two bodies and no way to call for help. Looks like we're going to have to figure out whodunnit ourselves before we end up like them." She gestured down at Adrian's corpse.

Timothy looked like he was going to be sick. Martha was whispering into her handbag. Ethan had a gleam in his eyes that bordered disquietingly on excitement, but this was his wheelhouse...sort of. And Bella was staring pensively at the pen sticking out of Adrian's chest.

Clary took a deep breath. "Okay, I know I'm a romance writer, not a detective, but it looks like I'm going to have to figure this out. We can't just sit around waiting to be picked off one by one."

The other authors nodded in agreement.

"I'll help. I did some research to write a book about a detective who's haunted after shooting an innocent person," said Ethan. As a horror writer, he was clearly no stranger to murder and mayhem. "That has to come in handy somehow, and two heads are better than one, right?"

Clary nodded, grateful for the assistance. In this bizarre situation, it was nice to have someone on her side even with limited experience.

"Great, you can be my partner in crime...solving," she said.

Ethan smiled, and their gazes locked in spite of the circumstances. "I like the sound of that."

They stood there a moment, the connection between them growing.

Clary broke the moment. "Okay, first step—examining the bodies for clues. Want to help me, partner?"

The others stood silently while she and Ethan examined Adrian. Not that they knew what they were looking for, but she agreed with Ethan's tentative theory that someone had stabbed him while he slept.

"I wonder about our murderer's obsession with writing implements?" she asked as she got to her feet with Ethan's assistance. The touch lingered a moment longer than necessary.

"Pens specifically," said Bella with a lack of inflection.

"If the murderer is an author, it makes sense they'd use the tools of the trade." Martha frowned. "I don't know anyone who writes longhand anymore though. Don't we all use laptops?"

"Dictation for me," said Timothy.

"To be fair, it's hard to stab someone with a laptop," said Clary with a weak chuckle. Ethan gave her a pity smile, but no one else responded.

"I guess we should..." She trailed off after a minute as she walked toward Adrian's door as Timothy covered him with a blanket. The others trailed behind, the group moving as one. Clary hoped against hope that between them, they could figure this out before the murderer struck again.

Chapter Four

BACK IN THE REC ROOM body, Clary and Ethan exchanged a look as the others hung back. "I think we need to question everyone," said Ethan in a low voice. "One of them has to be the killer."

Clary nodded reluctantly. She had grown to like her fellow authors over the past day. The thought that one was a murderer was hard to swallow. Raising her voice, she addressed the group. "I know this is uncomfortable, but we need to consider that the killer is among us."

Immediately there were exclamations of shock and denial.

"Surely you don't think it's one of us," said Martha, clutching her handbag.

"That's absurd," scoffed Timothy. "We're writers, not criminals."

Bella, in particular, seemed incensed. "How dare you accuse us? You have no proof."

Clary held up her hands placatingly. "I'm not accusing anyone specifically, but Brenna said we were the only ones on the island. So if she was telling the truth..."

"The murderer has to be one of us," said Ethan grimly.

Bella glared daggers at them. The others shifted uncomfortably, not meeting each other's eyes.

"No one is going outside in this storm to search for phantom intruders," said Clary, "So we have to assume, for now, the killer is in this room."

There were more protests, but less conviction behind them. The assembled writers eyed each other warily. The innocence of their retreat had been shattered. Someone among them was a bloodthirsty murderer with a penchant for irony and pens.

Clary decided to start questioning Martha. The cookbook author seemed the least threatening of the group. Taking Martha gently by the arm, Clary steered her into the kitchen. Once alone, she broke the tense silence. "Martha, did you have any...issues with Brenna?"

Martha shifted nervously, not meeting Clary's eyes. "We did disagree recently about my writing."

Clary nodded encouragingly. "Go on."

"She wanted me to jump on this gluten-free, keto, clean-eating train, but that's not me," Martha burst out. "I don't want to write diets and lifestyle books. I just want to write about comfort food and the recipes families have passed down for generations."

She finally met Clary's compassionate gaze. "Brenna said if I didn't get with the times, she'd cancel my contract." Her voice broke on a sob.

She laid a hand on her arm. "I'm so sorry she treated you that way, but surely you didn't...I mean, you wouldn't..."

Martha's eyes widened. "Of course not. Our disagreement was purely professional. I could never harm Brenna, no matter how cruel she was. She gave me my first contract."

Clary nodded, believing her. She squeezed Martha's arm reassuringly before heading back to the living room, the cookbook author trailing behind. One conversation down, and three to go.

As she returned to the living room, she realized she couldn't blindly assume Martha was being truthful. If she was going to pretend to be a detective, she'd have to think like one. If terrible TV shows had taught her anything, everyone on those was a liar—sometimes even the detectives in pursuit of the villain.

Ethan frowned when she returned. "You shouldn't go off alone with them. Let's interrogate them in the same room. I want to make sure you're safe."

A wave of warmth made her flush, but she tried to hide that response. A detective wouldn't be drooling over a prospective suspect, even if he was six-two, with thick, dark curls, and dreamy deep green eyes.

"Clary?"

She blinked at Bella calling her name, sounding impatient. She must have been woolgathering—or lusting after a potential murderer. Eek. She turned to the younger romance writer. "Yes?"

"I remember seeing Brenna's laptop upstairs. Should I go get it?"

She nodded. "Yes."

"No," said Ethan at the same time. He softened his tone at a glance from Clary. "Not alone, I mean. No one should go anywhere alone until we figure out..."

"Who among us took 'the pen is mightier than the sword' literally," said Clary with a shrill laugh, feeling giddy with horror for a second.

Ethan frowned but shrugged. "Right." He looked at Timothy. "Please go with her."

Timothy looked nervous, like he might stammer out an excuse to refuse, but then he squared his shoulders and seemed to assume a protective stance that was somewhat reminiscent of a mouse going up against a vulture as he gave Bella reassuring smile. "Let's get this done."

Bella and Timothy returned quickly, the young woman, with her nimble fingers and tech-savvy prowess, wasted no time in circumventing the laptop's security screen. Clary watched intently as the screen flickered to life, revealing the digital realm where Brenna's secrets might lie.

As Bella scrolled through the files, Clary's eyes widened at the sight of a document labeled "Author Considerations." "Stop. We should look at that."

As Bella clicked on it to open the document, a pang of apprehension tightened her stomach. The document contained a list of notes, each representing an author under scrutiny. Brenna had meticulously detailed her thoughts on dropping certain writers from her publishing empire, but the names were absent.

Clary's heart sank. The absence of specific names left her with more questions than answers. Had Brenna chosen to omit them deliberately? Or was it simply an oversight?

The remaining writers watched them intently, their gazes shifting nervously from Clary to Bella and back again. Clary couldn't ignore the underlying suspicion that now tainted their once harmonious gathering.

While Bella continued to peruse the laptop, Clary took a deep breath, ready to continue her investigation. She glanced at Martha, whose eyes were still red from their earlier conversation. She had to push her personal sympathy aside and focus on the task at hand.

"I appreciate your honesty earlier, but I need to know if there's anything else you can tell me. Any other possible motives or grievances with Brenna?" She tried to keep her expression aloof as she stared at the cookbook author.

Martha chewed her lip, deep in thought. "There is one thing... Brenna and I clashed over the promotion of my latest cookbook. She wanted me to do an extensive book tour, but I was hesitant. I didn't want to be away from my family for too long. My daughter's about to have her first baby, and..." She wrung her hands, looking helplessly torn.

Clary nodded, absorbing the information. Martha's reluctance to prioritize her writing career over her family's well-being was understandable, but would Brenna's pushback lead her to commit a heinous act? It seemed doubtful and unlikely from the charming middle-aged woman, but she couldn't be sure just yet.

As she prepared to move on to the next writer, her gaze met Ethan's. His concern for her safety had been evident earlier, but there was no room for distractions. She had to remain focused.

"Ethan," Clary said, her voice steady, "I'd like to ask you a few questions now. Please, share with me your thoughts on Brenna and anything that might help shed some light on this situation."

Ethan leaned forward, his eyes searching hers. "Brenna and I had our differences, no doubt. She often criticized my writing style, claiming it lacked the depth she sought for her publishing house. I don't think anyone really liked her, but I never thought it would come to this."

Clary observed Ethan's earnest expression, trying to discern any hint of deception. Was it possible he was playing a role, hiding something more sinister behind his surprised façade? She couldn't dismiss the thought entirely.

Clary turned her attention to Timothy, who had been quiet throughout their investigation so far. She noted the nervousness that still lingered in his eyes and the slight tremor in his hands. He seemed like he might bolt at any second, but there was a determination in his stance that piqued her curiosity.

She mustered a smile to put him at ease. "I'd like to hear your thoughts on Brenna. Did you have any encounters or disagreements with her that might shed light on our current predicament?"

Timothy's Adam's apple bobbed as he swallowed nervously. "Well, Brenna... she was a tough critic. She never held back her opinions about my self-help books. Always saying they lacked depth, and I was merely regurgitating clichés. It was disheartening, to say the least, but I think the real reason she disliked me is I'm still good friends with her ex-husband."

Clary felt a pang of sympathy for Timothy. As a fellow writer, she knew how harsh criticism could be and how it could chip away at one's confidence—especially coming from Brenna, who seemed to delight in being cruel rather than just blunt. Yet she had to remain impartial, to consider all possibilities. "I could see her being petty about something like that."

If she was going to be Detective Pretend, she had to dedicate herself to it. Too bad she wasn't required to write a swoon-worthy love scene instead of doing this. That, she could do in her sleep.

Clary refocused her attention on Timothy, her mind switching gears to her usual snarky and witty thought process. She couldn't help but wonder if Timothy's self-help expertise could offer any insights into their current predicament. Maybe he could write a book titled "Finding Clues and Channeling Inner Detectives For The Romance Writer."

"Where were you last night?"

He shrugged. "Mostly in my room writing. I did leave once to help myself to the snack table and encountered Brenna there, but that was maybe two hours after dinner?"

"While you were busy hammering away at your keyboard, did you happen to cross paths with anyone else or hear anything later that might shed light on our mysterious murder?"

Timothy rubbed his chin, pondering for a moment. "I heard the distant sound of thunderous footsteps, but I assumed it was just Bella on her third trip to the snack table. Other than that, it was eerily quiet."

Clary nodded. "That might have been when she was running away...if she was. Do you remember what time?"

He frowned. "I'm not sure. After midnight, I'd say, but I didn't look at the clock."

"That's okay."

With a nod, Timothy relaxed slightly, his initial nervousness giving way to a touch of humor. Clary was determined to maintain a lighter tone amidst the tension, using her playful banter to unravel the secrets that lay beneath their writerly façades.

Clary turned her attention to Ethan, feeling a twinge of guilt since they were unofficially partners in the investigation—unless he was murderer with a wicked sense of irony.

She mustered a sympathetic smile before diving into her next line of questioning. "Ethan, my partner in crime-solving, I'm sorry to put you in

32

the hot seat, but did you have any specific issues or disagreements with Brenna you didn't mention while ago?"

Ethan let out a sigh, his gaze briefly wandering before meeting Clary's eyes. "Brenna and I had a bit of a clash over the direction of my latest novel. She thought the plot lacked excitement and urged me to sprinkle in some dramatic twists. I, being the stubborn writer that I am, insisted on staying true to my artistic vision. It created some...shall we say, literary fireworks between us."

Clary nodded, mentally imagining the clash of literary titans. It was like a battle of pens with ink flying everywhere. She couldn't help but smile at the absurdity of the image before her smile disappeared when she recalled just how deadly a pen could be in the wrong hands.

"I have to ask again for clarity... During the time of the murder, you mentioned you were in the shower. Can anyone vouch for your whereabouts?"

Ethan's brow furrowed as he pondered for a moment. "No one actually saw me in the shower unless there's a peeping tom ghost around, but that's where I was, I swear. The steam and hot water are my secret ingredients for creative inspiration. It's like a mini sauna for my brain."

"I totally get it," said Clary, her voice laced with understanding. "I appreciate your honesty, even if your alibi is as steamy as my plotlines."

As she looked into Ethan's eyes, she caught a glimpse of earnestness mixed with a hint of uncertainty. There was something more lurking beneath the surface, and she made a mental note to dig deeper.

Clary turned her attention to Bella, ready to ask her the next round of questions. However, before she could utter a word, Bella preempted her, her tone laced with defiance and frustration.

"Hold up, Detective Clary," Bella interjected, crossing her arms. "Before we continue this little interrogation game, I want to know what your deal is. What's your issue with Brenna? It's pretty obvious that we're all here because she had an ax to grind with each of us, at least professionally."

Clary raised an eyebrow, momentarily caught off-guard by Bella's directness. She couldn't deny the truth in Bella's words. They were all connected by their tangled web of writerly conflicts with Brenna. It was like a twisted anthology of grievances.

With a wry smile, Clary met Bella's gaze. "Touché, Bella. You've certainly hit the nail on the head. Brenna had her fair share of clashes with each of us, and that's precisely why we're here, trying to untangle this murder mystery. As for my personal failing...Brenna was getting frustrated with my bouts of writer's block and missing deadlines. She was relentless in her pursuit of me finishing my next novel, as if she had a personal vendetta against my procrastination."

Bella's eyebrows shot up in surprise, her defiant expression softening a bit. "So, you were one of her targets too?"

"Of course. As you said, I think Brenna had something against all of us." She took a deep breath. "Now, about you and—"

Bella's expression hardened. She crossed her arms and shook her head. "I'm not doing this. I'm not going to play detective and interrogate my friends, or pretend you know what the heck you're doing. I'll wait until the real detectives arrive." With that, she turned on her heel and stormed off, leaving a trail of frustration in her wake.

Clary watched Bella's departure with a sigh. She couldn't blame Bella for feeling overwhelmed by the situation. It was a lot to handle, and not everyone had the temperament for amateur sleuthing. Not that she did either, but with a lack of candidates, someone had to take the reins.

Before Clary could react, Timothy sprang into action, chasing after Bella. He called out her name, his voice filled with genuine worry. "Bella, wait, I'll come with you. You shouldn't be alone in this."

Clary noticed the underlying tenderness in Timothy's voice as he rushed to Bella's side. There was more than just concern for her safety. It seemed that he had developed a fondness for her. She hoped it was more paternal than something else, considering he must have twenty years on the young author.

"I could use some sleep," said Martha quietly.

"Me too." Ethan bit back a yawn. "We should sleep together."

Her heart skipped a beat as she briefly contemplated it before realizing Ethan was staring at her and Martha. "Huh?"

He frowned. "In the same room for safety. I don't think anyone should be alone."

She nodded, pretending she'd understood his intention from the start and wasn't disappointed he hadn't been propositioning her. She cleared her throat. "I think there's a king-size in Brenna's room."

"That'll work," said Ethan. Martha nodded after a moment, and they walked upstairs together.

As they entered Brenna's room moments later, the largest one with a king-size bed, she said, "We should see if there are any clues here before we mess it up by sleeping."

Ethan nodded, his gaze scanning the room. "Agreed. Let's take a closer look to search for any clues."

"Like what?" asked Martha.

Clary shrugged. "Anything out of the ordinary."

The cookbook author snorted but started searching through the drawers. As they meticulously examined every nook and cranny, Clary's mind wandered to the whimsical possibilities. She imagined hidden compartments behind ornate mirrors, secret passages disguised as bookshelves, and a treasure trove of unpublished manuscripts waiting to be discovered.

"Ah, the joys of being an eccentric writer," Clary mused, her voice filled with a mix of sarcasm and wonder. "One minute, we're struggling with writer's block, and the next, we're imagining secret lairs and unraveling murder mysteries. Who needs ordinary lives when we have all this excitement?"

Ethan chuckled, his eyes twinkling. "You do have a way of finding the extraordinary in the ordinary, Clary. It's a gift."

Clary shrugged, a playful smirk on her face. "Call it a writer's curse, always seeing stories where others see mundane realities. But let's focus on the task at hand."

"Why bother?" Martha sounded defeated. "We don't even know what we're looking for here." She looked up then. "Maybe we should explore the rest of the island tomorrow. Who knows what we might stumble upon?"

Clary nodded, her mind buzzing with anticipation. "Tomorrow, but for now, let's try to get some rest. Our tangled tales await us in the morning, and we'll need all the wit and imagination we can muster."

As a group, they settled into their respective spots on the bed, and Martha's light snores soon filled the room.

"I can't help thinking her husband might appreciate her going on a book tour so he can get a few nights of sleep without that noise," said Ethan with a small laugh.

"It's not that bad. My ex-fiancé snored so much worse. What about you?"

"I've never snored in my life."

Clary snorted. "Sure you haven't. I was asking about your current...former...whatever's snoring tendencies?" So smooth. She might as well have just blatantly asked if he was single. It couldn't have been worse than that.

There was a smile in his voice. "No current, and it's been a long time since I had a former. It's hard to find someone who understands my writing schedule."

She sighed with envy. "I wish I could stick to a schedule."

He laughed. "That's the problem. I sometimes spend eighteen hours writing and three days resting and preparing to write again. It's hard with a normal nine to fiver."

"I understand. My sister lives that way, but I can't imagine being so tied down and stuck on the same schedule every day."

"Is that why you and the ex-fiancé didn't make it down the aisle?"

"No." She waited for a pang of regret that didn't come. "Stuart was too busy chasing anything in a skirt to bother getting married. I'm just glad I realized it before I bought a dress and started booking venues. He liked the idea of being married to a famous bestselling author but didn't want to give up the perks of being single, like banging his secretary."

"What a cad. Should I write him in my next book as a victim?"

She grinned. "Yes, please." That made her think of Brenna though, and she shivered. "She really was a horrible person."

"Brenna? Yeah."

"Still, that's cold—a red pen through the heart."

"Yeah. It's hard to imagine it's one of us who killed her." He sounded uncomfortable. "I prefer to write creepy, atmospheric horror over living it."

"I'd rather write about falling madly in love and having amazing orgasms." She let out a startled yelp as she said that, wondering what happened to her admittedly already-weak filter.

He sounded intrigued. "Are you writing based on real-life?"

She snorted. "Not with Stuart the Skirt-chaser."

"That's too bad." His tone had turned intimate. "You deserve to have that."

"Falling madly in love?" Her throat was dry, but her palms were sweaty as her heart kicked it up a notch to beat faster.

After a deliberate pause, he said, "That too," in a smoky tone.

He was definitely flirting with her. The giddy girl inside was absolutely swooning at the idea, but it was warring with the newly risen detective, who was trying to remind her he might be trying to seduce her away from considering him a suspect.

Go to sleep, damned detective, she thought sternly to herself, wanting to enjoy the moment of fantasizing about Ethan not being a murderer without reality intruding.

Chapter Five

THE DISCORDANT CACOPHONY of raised voices greeted Clary like an airhorn to the eardrums first thing in the morning. She blearily opened one eye, then the other, the fog of sleep slowly receding. She sat up, realizing she had Brenna's bed to herself, but raised voices came from the second floor.

Clary groaned. It was too early for hysterics without coffee. Sliding out from beneath the covers, she briefly contemplated smothering herself with a pillow. Maybe she'd get lucky and it would be a murder-suicide by Egyptian cotton. Instead, she got out of bed and followed them to a sitting room across the hall.

"I knew it was fishy how chipper you were after Brenna snuffed it." Martha's usually dulcet tone was several octaves too high. "Admit it, you did the old girl in."

"How dare you?" Bella's voice hit a pitch audible only to nearby canines. "I'll sue for slander!"

Martha and Bella squared off like two rival boxers fresh from the corners. A worried-looking Timothy wrung his hands nearby. Meanwhile, Ethan leaned against the wall, observing the drama with a bemused look.

"Good morning to you too," said Clary. Drawing herself up, she loudly clapped her hands. "Enough! You're giving me a migraine."

Three heads swiveled her way, surprise splashed across their faces like paint on a canvas.

Clary massaged her temples. "It's too early for accusations. Let's make coffee and try to be civilized human beings, shall we?"

The others exchanged sheepish looks. Martha and Bella retreated to neutral corners while they trooped downstairs as a group. Once on the first floor, Timothy scurried to the kitchen in search of caffeine.

As Margaret went to the fridge, and the rich aroma of brewing coffee filled the air, Clary turned to Ethan. "This day is off to a roaring start." She rubbed her ears, which still rang. "Literally."

He smirked. "Just another relaxing retreat morning." His grin faded. "But Martha had a good idea before you woke up. We should re-examine the body for any clues we might have missed earlier."

Clary nodded, the remaining grogginess burned away by the spike of adrenaline. She hadn't considered checking Brenna's corpse again, but Ethan was right that the extra scrutiny could reveal something vital.

Moments later, the authors were gathered somberly around their former editor's body splayed out on the divan with Martha clutching her tub of yogurt like it was a talisman. Clary gritted her teeth against the assault of bodily odors one didn't encounter outside of a real morgue. How in the world was Martha continuing to eat yogurt with that stench?

She forced herself to take in every detail, watching Ethan closely as he did the same. His fingers traced the air just above Brenna's waxy skin before pausing at her right hand. She grasped a familiar piece of jewelry tightly in her purple-tinged fingers.

A gasp tore from Clary's throat. It was her bracelet, the one Emily had given her last birthday, to commemorate the big three-oh. Heart pounding, she unconsciously rubbed her now-bare wrist. She'd worn it yesterday and left it on the dresser in her room last night after seeing Brenna's body. It has been there while she slept in Brenna's room with the others, but would they believe her?

Ethan gently extracted the bracelet, examining it closely, then locked eyes with Clary. "I think we just found our first real piece of evidence." He sounded almost regretful.

Clary stood utterly dumbfounded as the others gaped at the bracelet, then back at her, eyes wide as.

Martha's spoon clattered to the floor, yogurt dripping unheeded. "You...you killed her." She gasped, pointing a trembling finger at Clary. The accusation wounded Clary like a sucker punch to the stomach. She stumbled back, hands raised beseechingly. "What? No! I swear I didn't—"

"Save it," said Martha. "That's your bracelet, isn't it? Caught red-handed!"

Clary blinked helplessly, her mind scrambling for purchase like a cat on linoleum. How could she possibly explain the inexplicable?

"Now, hold on," said Ethan, ever her knight in slightly rumpled armor. "There has to be an explanation."

Martha was having none of it. Her face flushed an alarming crimson as she jabbed an accusatory finger at Clary again and again, like a woodpecker drilling outrage into an oak. "Of all the sneaky, underhanded tricks...pretending to help investigate when you're the killer." Martha shook with righteous fury, yogurt abandoned. "Admit what you've done."

Clary's heartbeat whooshed in her ears, drowning out all else. The room tilted dangerously as shocked disbelief gave way to panicked despair. It was her bracelet clutched in the victim's death grip. How could she possibly prove her innocence now?

She swayed on her feet, the walls undulating like a funhouse. This couldn't be happening. She was no killer, just a romance writer with a sassy cat and a penchant for tea and late-night ice cream.

Amidst the dizzying vortex of confusion, she latched onto the one anchor keeping her from spinning out to sea—Ethan. Dear, steadfast Ethan, gazing at her with those penetrating green eyes that seized her very soul.

"I didn't..." She croaked, her gaze beseeching him to understand.

His jaw set in determination, Ethan stepped forward, exuding an air of calm authority. "Everyone, just take a breath. Clary isn't a killer."

But the others weren't placated so easily. Martha's sausage-like finger was back to wagging in Clary's face like she was reprimanding a naughty pup.

"The only explanation is that she's guilty. Just look at her bracelet right there in Brenna's cold dead hand," Martha said shrilly.

And she had a point, darn it. That bracelet was Clary's albatross now, the evidence she couldn't refute. Still, Ethan held his ground, bless him.

"Maybe someone planted it there. We don't know anything for certain yet—" He tried reasoning, but Martha cut him off.

"Open your eyes. It's plain as day, and you're just too smitten to see it." She whirled on Clary again. "Confess, you backstabbing murderer!"

Clary flinched as if slapped. Smitten? Surely Martha was mistaken...or was she?

Now wasn't the time for swooning, not with Martha shrieking for her head on a pike. She held up her hands pleadingly as Martha advanced, finger at the ready. "Please, listen to me. I didn't kill anyone."

Unmoved, Martha opened her mouth to retort, but Ethan intervened. "That's enough." He gently pulled her aside, away from Martha's finger-jabbing fury. "We need to handle this calmly."

Clary nearly wilted with relief and gratitude. She managed a tremulous smile. "Thank you for believing in me when no one else does."

Ethan gave her shoulder a reassuring squeeze. "Of course, but we need to figure out how your bracelet ended up on the body." He paused, hesitating. "Where were you last night, exactly?"

Clary tensed. She'd been in her room, alone. No one could corroborate her story. Licking dry lips, she met Ethan's probing gaze. "I was in my room all night until I woke up and saw Brenna. Then I found you in the hallway, and everything else unfolded. I wasn't alone at any point after that, and the bracelet was in my room. I swear on my lazy feline life companion that I didn't kill anyone."

Ethan studied her intently before giving a brisk nod. "All right. Without proof either way, we have to keep investigating, but this does complicate things."

Doubt still perfumed the air as pungently as Martha's spilled yogurt and Brenna's presence, but Clary clung to the fraying lifeline of Ethan's trust. Somehow, someway, she had to clear her name before suspicion drowned her entirely.

Chapter Six

A BLOODCURDLING SCREAM rent the air, scattering Clary's thoughts like dandelion seeds in the wind. She exchanged an alarmed glance with Ethan before they both dashed upstairs, taking the rickety steps two at a time.

They arrived panting in the second-floor hallway to find Bella sprawled dramatically across the faded oriental rug. Overhead, the crystal chandelier swayed gently, as if caught in a phantom breeze. Part of it was missing, and it hung awkwardly askew.

"Are you all right?" Clary rushed to give her a quick once-over for injuries.

Bella, however, seemed more interested in the drama of the moment than any potential bodily harm. She was sprawled on the floor like a damsel in a Victorian melodrama, her hand dramatically pressed to her forehead.

With a whimper, Bella pointed a trembling, manicured finger upward. "It almost crushed me." Her voice was shaky, but her eyes were alight with a strange excitement.

Following her gaze, Clary noted the chandelier's missing crystals and askew chains. Parts of it had crashed to the floor at least three feet from the woman. She gave Bella a sympathetic pat, hiding her skepticism. The young author seemed oddly composed for someone nearly flattened like a pancake.

Ethan moved to inspect the chandelier, climbing on an end table that he dragged a few feet closer first. He was frowning, his eyes narrowed in concentration. "These cables were cut. The chandelier didn't just happen to fall. This was intentional."

Clary's pulse quickened as the realization sank in. This had been no household accident. Someone had deliberately tampered with the chandelier to send the hovering ornament crashing down like a crystal guillotine.

She exchanged a meaningful look with Ethan, reading the same conclusion in his gaze. They had a cold-blooded killer in their midst, and whoever it was had no qualms about claiming more victims.

With the revelation of the cut cables, the atmosphere in the house shifted from uneasy to downright tense. At Ethan's suggestion of regrouping, they all trooped into Brenna's office moments later, the room seeming to shrink under the weight of their collective anxiety.

Ethan was the first to break the silence. "We need to figure out what's going on," he said, his voice steady despite the circumstances. "We're all in danger here."

Bella, still pale from her near-death experience, shook her head. "I can't," she said, her voice barely a whisper. "I just need... I need some time."

Martha, who had been silent until now, nodded. "We understand, Bella. You take your time."

With Bella's departure, the remaining authors turned their attention to Brenna's office. It was a mess of papers and coffee stains. They began to sift through the papers, their hearts pounding in their chests.

Among the clutter, a folder caught Clary's eye. It was labeled "Sales Figures: Romance" and inside were documents comparing Bella and Clary's book sales. Brenna's notes were scrawled in the margins, her sharp words cutting even in death.

"Bella will never cut it," one note read. *"Clary is the real talent here."*

Clary felt a pang of sympathy for Bella. Despite her ambition and drive, Brenna had clearly not believed in her, but was that enough to drive Bella to murder? Or was she just another pawn in this deadly game?

As they pondered the implications, Martha's gaze kept drifting back to Clary. It was a speculative look, one that made Clary's skin crawl. She could well imagine Martha was mentally trying to figure out how she'd killed Brenna and slipped back in to "discover" her after sabotaging the boat and then the radio inside. If Martha wrote fiction, she'd easily see this was far too obvious, and Clary couldn't be the murderer. If life were a novel.

As they continued their search, Timothy unearthed a letter tucked away in a drawer. It was addressed to Bella, but it didn't seem that it had ever been sent. As he read it aloud, the room fell silent.

"Bella," he began, his voice shaking slightly, *"I regret to inform you that due to the poor quality of your writing and the lackluster sales of your recent books, I have decided to terminate our professional relationship."*

He looked up, his eyes meeting Clary's. "Brenna was planning to drop Bella."

A heavy silence filled the room. Clary could see the shock on Ethan's face and the sympathy in Martha's eyes, but it was Timothy's reaction that caught her attention. He looked unsurprised.

"Brenna probably changed her mind about mailing it and decided to tell her in person." His voice was barely above a whisper. "She had a way of crushing you and making you feel like you were nothing."

Clary nodded. She knew all too well how Brenna could be, but they also needed to stay focused. They were still trapped on an island with a murderer, and they needed to figure out who it was before it was too late.

As they continued to sift through Brenna's office, Clary's mind was racing. "Okay, let's start by questioning everyone separately again," she said moments later, when they didn't find anything useful. Without a neon sign proclaiming it was a clue, they really didn't know what to look for anyway.

Timothy grimaced. "Why? You don't know what you're doing."

She glared at him. "Do you have any better ideas?"

The self-help author shuffled his feet and looked away.

Martha sniffed at Clary. "I'm not sure I trust you."

Ignoring her, Ethan nodded in agreement. "Sounds like a plan. Let's see if we can get to the bottom of this."

As they prepared to dive into their investigation, Timothy startled her. He removed his glasses, blinking rapidly. "You should talk to me first. There's something I need to tell you."

Chapter Seven

STUNNED SILENCE MET Timothy's announcement. Martha, who had been eyeing Clary with suspicion, now turned her gaze to Timothy. Her eyes were wide, her mouth a thin line.

Ethan, meanwhile, was staring at Timothy with a thoughtful expression. His fingers tapped a rhythm on the top of Brenna's desk, like indicating his mind was working overtime.

He took a deep breath, steadying himself as he polished his glasses before putting them on again. "After dinner on our first night, Brenna pulled me aside. She said my sales were too dreadful to continue our working relationship, and she was dropping me." His mouth twisted. "She suggested I ask John to publish me knowing full well he took the fantasy and SF division and doesn't do nonfiction."

A gasp echoed through the room.

"John?" Martha frowned.

"Her ex-husband...the one who took half the publishing empire when they split last year, and I dared remain friends with him." Timothy sounded unconcerned about having committed such a grievous sin, at least in Brenna's eyes. "She was so cold when she told me."

Clary winced on his behalf. He was a gentle soul, and his self-help books were a reflection of his kind heart. To be dropped by Brenna, especially in such a cruel manner, must have been a devastating blow.

"She had me travel all this way just so she could sever ties in person," Timothy continued, his voice barely above a whisper. "She wanted to see my reaction. I knew she never liked me, but it was so cruel of her to enjoy watching me suffer and squirm. I think she wanted me to beg." He squared his shoulders with quiet dignity. "I refused to give her the satisfaction."

The room was silent as they absorbed the revelation. A chill ran down her spine. Brenna's cruelty knew no bounds, but was it enough to drive someone to murder? She glanced at Timothy, his face pale and drawn. Could he have killed Brenna out of anger and humiliation?

Timothy's confession hung in the air, a tangible cloud of despair and anger. Clary moved to Brenna's desk. She began to sift through the papers, her eyes scanning for any clue that could shed light on Timothy's claims.

Among the clutter, she found another folder labeled "Sales Figures: Timothy Small." Inside were documents that painted a different picture from what Brenna had told Timothy. "These documents show your sales weren't poor, Timothy," said Clary, holding up the papers. "In fact, they were quite good. Definitely solid mid-lister. Brenna lied to you."

Timothy looked up, his eyes wide with shock. "She... she lied?" His voice was barely a whisper as the words seemed to take all his strength to utter.

Clary nodded, her heart aching for the man. "She lied to justify her decision to drop you, probably because you didn't turn on John as she expected." She was glad she'd never become friendly with John or Brenna and hadn't been expected to pick a side—though she doubted that expectation was on John's side. He'd always struck her as calm and steady, and she wondered how he'd endured marriage to Brenna for ten years.

The room was silent as they absorbed this revelation. Timothy's face was a mask of shock and hurt, his eyes glistening with unshed tears. "I almost begged her to reconsider," he admitted, his voice barely a whisper. "I was so angry... so desperate..."

His words hung heavy in the air, a confession of sorts. Clary watched him, her mind whirling. Could gentle, kind-hearted Timothy have killed Brenna in a fit of rage?

It was as though he'd read Clary's thoughts. "I hated her," said Timothy, his voice breaking. "I hated her so much, but I didn't kill her. I swear."

The room was soundless as they absorbed his words. Martha, who had been silent throughout Timothy's confession, finally spoke. "I think we all need some time to process this," she said, her voice shaky. She gave Timothy a compassionate look before leaving the room, her footsteps echoing in the silence.

Timothy, looking like a man who had just had his world shattered, slowly rose from his seat. He gave Clary a nod and mouthed a silent thank you before leaving the room.

Once they were alone, Ethan turned to Clary. "Timothy's desperation makes him a credible suspect," he said, his voice low. "We need to keep an eye on him."

Clary nodded, her mind racing. "We should find Bella next," she said, her voice steady despite the turmoil inside her.

Ethan agreed, and they left Brenna's office with the room now feeling more like a crime scene than a workspace. As they walked down the hallway, the house seemed eerily quiet, the storm outside the only sound filling the silence.

They didn't find Bella in her room or in the living room. Instead, they found Martha in the kitchen, her back to them as she busied herself making tea. She jumped when they entered, her hand flying to her chest.

"Oh, you startled me," she said, her voice shaky. She quickly composed herself, turning to face them with a tight smile. "Can I offer you some tea?"

Clary exchanged a glance with Ethan. They had come looking for Bella, but perhaps it was time to question Martha again instead. After all, everyone was a suspect until proven innocent. And as they had just learned, even the most unlikely of people could harbor deep-seated resentment and desperation.

"Sure, Martha," said Clary, taking a seat at the kitchen table. "Tea sounds great. And while we're here, maybe we can chat a bit."

Chapter Eight

SHE TURNED TO FACE them, her face a mask of calm. "I figured as much," she said, her voice steady. "What do you want to know?"

"We need to know if there was anything... anything else at all that you haven't told us that could have caused tension between you two."

Martha was silent for a moment, her gaze focused on the teapot in front of her. "Brenna and I... We had our differences. She wanted me to write about trendier things, like keto or gluten-free. And she was pushing for a big book tour that would take me away from my family."

"As you've mentioned, but there was something else, wasn't there?" asked Ethan, his voice soft. "Something more personal?"

Martha sighed, her shoulders slumping. "Yes," she said, her voice barely above a whisper. "There was something else."

She took a deep breath, her hands gripping the edge of the counter. "When I was younger, I... I made some mistakes." Her voice was barely above a whisper. "I was desperate for money and for fame. I thought I could find it in Hollywood."

She paused, her gaze distant. "I ended up in an adult film," she confessed, her voice shaking. "It was a one-time thing, under a fake name. I thought it was well buried in the past when I returned home a year or so later, deciding Georgia was where I wanted to be."

"But Brenna found out," Ethan finished for her, his voice soft.

"My husband is a pastor. You have no idea the scandal..." She trailed off with a sniff.

"I can imagine. What did she want from you?" asked Clary.

Her eyes welled with tears. "She was using the information to force me to take no advance, a lower royalty, and do a big book tour with my next release." She drew in a shaky breath, and her lips curved into a tentative smile that quickly faded. "With her gone, I'm finally free from her threats."

The confession hung in the air, a tangible cloud of regret and relief. The room was silent as they absorbed the revelation. Clary's heart ached for Martha. Despite her past mistakes, she had built a life for herself with a family, and Brenna had threatened to take it all away.

"But I didn't kill her," said Martha, her voice firm. "I hated her for what she was doing, but I didn't kill her."

Clary nodded, her mind racing. Martha had a motive, that was clear, but did she have the guts to commit murder? And where did that leave them in their investigation?

Ethan, who had been silent throughout Martha's confession, finally spoke. "We need to keep looking," he said, his voice steady. "There has to be something we're missing."

Clary agreed. "Let's split up and see if anything else stands out to us. We can regroup in an hour."

He frowned. "I don't like splitting up."

She nodded. "But we'll cover more ground."

With a reluctant nod, he stood up and gestured for her to precede him. They left Martha in the kitchen, each lost in their own thoughts. The house seemed eerier now, the shadows darker, but she couldn't afford to let fear get the best of her. They had a mystery to solve, and a killer to catch.

Chapter Nine

CLARY'S HEART POUNDED in her chest as she moved through the house, her mind a whirl of thoughts and theories. The house was eerily silent, the only sound the creaking of the old wooden floors under her feet and the wind howling outside.

As she entered the library, a room filled with towering bookshelves and the scent of old paper, she felt a strange sense of unease. Libraries were usually soothing, but this place made even the most hallowed sanctuary seem corrupt. She moved through the room, her fingers trailing over the spines of the books. Suddenly, she stumbled, her foot catching on a loose floorboard. She reached out to steady herself, and her hand landed on a bookshelf.

To her surprise, the bookshelf moved, exposing it also served as a hidden door. Her heart pounding, she pushed open the door/shelf, revealing a hidden office. It was a stark contrast to the rest of the house, modern and sleek with a large desk and state-of-the-art computer.

As she moved through the room, she realized this was Brenna's real office. The woman had lived on the island, not just rented it for the retreat as they'd assumed. Why have a secret office though?

She soon discerned the reason Brenna wanted to keep this area hidden. The office was a treasure trove of secrets, each one more shocking than the last. Clary moved to the desk, her fingers trembling as she opened the drawers and looked through files. Inside one of the filing cabinet drawers, she found a box labeled "M. Masterson." With a sense of dread, she opened it, revealing a DVD case. The cover was a still from an adult film, and there, in the corner, was a young woman who bore a striking resemblance to Martha.

Poor Martha. This was the secret Brenna had held over her, the threat that had kept her in line. She heard footsteps and quickly closed the box before she turned to see Ethan standing in the doorway.

His eyes widened as he took in the room. "What is this place?" he asked, his voice barely above a whisper.

"Brenna's real office," said Clary, her voice shaky. "I think she was living here on the island."

"Huh. I thought she'd just rented it for this creepy retreat." Ethan moved to join her, his eyes scanning the room. He picked up a stack of papers from the desk, his brows furrowing as he read. "These are contracts," he said, his voice filled with disbelief. "Blackmail contracts."

Clary moved closer, her eyes scanning the documents. Each one was more shocking than the last. "Look at this one," she said, pointing to a contract with the name "Jay Sunders" on it. "I know his name. He's a famous thriller writer. Brenna was forcing him to give up half his royalties in exchange for her silence about..." She looked through the file for a second. "An affair."

Ethan whistled, shaking his head. "And this one," he said, holding up another contract, "Ynez Santos, that popstar with her biography that took off like a bullet, was being blackmailed into making unpaid appearances at Brenna's events. She threatened to reveal...a past arrest for drug possession. That could ruin Ynez since she projects such a wholesome image."

They continued to sift through the documents, each one revealing another piece of Brenna's intricate web of manipulation. It was clear Brenna had been running a blackmail empire under the guise of a publishing house.

As they delved deeper into the documents, they found more and more evidence of Brenna's illicit dealings. There were letters threatening to reveal secrets, contracts demanding money or services, and even photographs that could ruin careers.

The more they discovered, the more they realized how little they had truly known about Brenna. She had been a master manipulator, pulling the strings behind the scenes and keeping her authors in line with threats and blackmail.

"I can't believe it," said Ethan, running a hand through his hair. "We knew she was tough, even ruthless at times, but this is something else."

Clary nodded, her mind racing. "We respected her as an editor, but she was never our friend. She was always so harsh. Yet this is beyond anything I could have imagined."

Ethan sighed, rubbing his temples. "And to think we were all just pawns in her game. She was manipulating us for her own gain."

"That's basically publishing," she said with a small smile that faded. "Blackmail isn't though." Clary's heart ached for her fellow authors. They had all been victims of Brenna's manipulation. They had trusted her with their careers, their dreams, and she had used that trust to exploit them.

"We need to tell the others," said Clary, her voice firm. She picked up the box that rightfully belonged to Martha when her fingers brushed against the cold metal. "And we need to return this to Martha."

Ethan nodded, his expression grim. "You're right. Let's go."

They left Brenna's secret office, the door/bookshelf closing with a soft click behind them. The house was eerily quiet, the silence broken only by their muted footsteps. They made their way to the rec room, where they found Timothy and Martha engaged in quiet conversation.

"Guys," said Clary, her voice echoing in the large room. "We found something."

Timothy and Martha turned to look at them, their expressions filled with curiosity and apprehension. Clary took a deep breath, steeling herself for the conversation to come. She held the box behind her back, out of sight.

"We found Brenna's real office," Ethan began, his voice steady. "And we found evidence Brenna was blackmailing authors. Using their secrets against them."

The room fell silent as Timothy and Martha absorbed the news. Shock, disbelief, and finally, acceptance—much faster in Martha's case—flickered across their faces.

As the news sank in, Clary moved closer to Martha. She discreetly handed her the box, their eyes meeting in a silent exchange. As Clary gave the box to Martha, she saw a change in the older woman's eyes. The suspicion that had been there before seemed to soften, replaced by a flicker of gratitude. Martha took the box, her fingers brushing against Clary's in a silent thank you.

"But where's Bella?" asked Martha, her voice barely above a whisper. "She needs to know about this."

"We don't know. We've been looking for her, but she's nowhere to be found," said Ethan.

The room was silent as they absorbed the news. Bella was missing, Brenna had been blackmailing some of them, and they were all suspects in a murder investigation. It was like a plot from one of their novels, but this was all too real, and they were right in the middle of it.

Ethan's gaze was fixed on the window, the storm outside casting a gloomy shadow over his features. "We need to find Bella," he said, his voice carrying a weight of determination. "She's been missing for too long."

Timothy and Martha exchanged a glance, their faces mirroring the same apprehension. "In this weather?" asked Timothy, his voice barely above a whisper. The storm outside was raging, the wind howling like a beast in the night.

Ethan nodded, his jaw set. "We can't just sit here. Bella could be in danger."

Clary rose from her seat, her heart pounding in her chest. "I'll go with you," she said. Bella was a drama queen, but even she wouldn't disappear without a word in the middle of a storm.

Ethan gave her a grateful nod. "I need to grab a sweater from my room. It's freezing out there."

They made their way to Ethan's room, the house silent around them. As Ethan opened his suitcase, a stack of letters tumbled out onto the floor. Clary bent down to pick them up, her breath hitching as she recognized Brenna's handwriting. "What are these?"

Ethan turned, his face paling as he saw the letters in her hand. He reached out to take them, but Clary pulled back, her eyes meeting his. "What are these, Ethan?" she repeated, her voice firm.

"They're nothing," said Ethan too quickly. His eyes were wide with a hint of panic in them.

Clary wasn't convinced. She held up one of the letters, her heart pounding in her chest. "This is Brenna's handwriting," she said, her voice barely above a whisper. She sniffed the ornate pink envelopes edged with gold, and they smelled like the editor's perfume. They had to be... "Why do you have love letters from Brenna?"

Ethan's face was a mask of shame. He opened his mouth to speak, but no words came out. He looked like a man cornered, his eyes darting around the room as if looking for an escape.

Clary felt a pang of betrayal. She had trusted Ethan and had started to develop feelings for him. And all the while, he had been hiding this from her. She felt a lump form in her throat, her eyes stinging with unshed tears.

"I deserve an explanation," she said, her voice steady despite the turmoil inside her. She held his gaze, waiting for him to speak. A chilling thought crept into her mind. Could Ethan have killed Brenna? Was it possible that the man she had started to care for was capable of such a heinous act?

A wave of nausea washed over her. She took a step back, her hand instinctively reaching for the door handle behind her. She needed to get out, to breathe, to think.

Ethan seemed to sense her distress. "Clary, wait," he said, his voice pleading. "Let me explain."

Clary paused, her hand still on the door handle. She turned to face him, her heart pounding in her chest. "Start talking."

Ethan took a deep breath, his gaze never leaving hers. "She developed an infatuation with me after she became convinced the heroine in my last novel was based on her." He snorted. "In truth, every villain is based on Brenna, but she started sending me these letters. I never encouraged her. I never reciprocated her feelings."

Clary felt sympathy, but it was quickly overshadowed by her confusion and hurt. "Why didn't you tell me?" she asked, her voice barely a whisper.

"I was going to," said Ethan, his voice filled with regret. "I brought the letters here to confront her, to tell her to stop. I was even considering cutting ties with the publishing company and going independent."

Clary was silent, her mind a whirl of thoughts and emotions. She didn't know what to believe. She needed time to process everything. "I... I need to think," she said, her voice shaky. Tossing the letters at his bed, she turned and left the room, leaving Ethan alone with his letters and his guilt.

As she made her way downstairs, she spotted Bella in the kitchen. She was alone, her face pale and drawn. She needed to talk to her, to get her side of the story, but first, she needed to clear her head, to make sense of the revelations about Ethan. She was no longer sure who she could trust, and that was a terrifying thought.

Chapter Ten

BELLA HAD HER BACK to the door as she stared out the window at the storm raging outside. The room was filled with the scent of coffee, a stark contrast to the tension that hung in the air.

"We need to talk."

Bella turned, her eyes guarded. "About what?" she asked, her voice defensive.

"About Brenna," said Clary, meeting Bella's gaze. "About your relationship with her."

Bella's face hardened, her lips pressing into a thin line. "What about it?" she asked, her voice cold.

She held her gaze, her heart pounding in her chest. "It seems like there was some tension between the two of you."

Bella scoffed, crossing her arms over her chest. "Tension? Is that what you're calling it?"

"So, there was a problem?"

Bella was silent for a moment, her gaze focused on Clary. "Brenna and my mother were childhood friends," she said, her voice barely above a whisper. "That's why she gave me a shot in the first place, but she was always pushing me, always expecting more."

"And did that lead to a falling-out?" asked Clary, her voice soft.

Bella's gaze dropped to the floor, her hands clenched at her sides. "She was going to replace you," she said, her voice shaky. "She was grooming me to take over for you, Clary, saying you were losing your audience and weren't reliable with missing deadlines. Then she decided I wasn't good enough."

Clary winced. She'd realized Brenna was impatient with her lapses but hadn't realized she was trying to replace her in the romance market. It hurt, but she had to acknowledge she'd had problems writing the last couple of years. It had started with Stuart, when she'd realized love wasn't enough and might not even really exist.

"She was going to drop you?" she asked, trying to keep her voice steady. Inside, she wanted to ask how soon Brenna had planned to drop *her* too.

Bella nodded, her eyes filled with a mix of anger and hurt. "She said I wasn't ready, that I needed more time, but I knew what she really meant. She didn't think I was good enough."

"And how did that make you feel?" asked Clary, her mind racing. This was a motive, a strong one, but was it enough to drive Bella to murder?

Bella's laugh was bitter. "How do you think it made me feel? I was furious. I felt betrayed. But I didn't kill her, if that's what you're implying."

Clary held up her hands in a placating gesture. "I'm not accusing you. I'm just trying to understand."

Bella's gaze was hard, but she nodded. "Fine. Understand this. I didn't kill Brenna. I hated her, yes, but I didn't kill her."

Clary nodded, her mind whirling. Bella had a motive, that was clear, but would she commit murder? And where did that leave them in their investigation?

As she left Bella, Clary decided she'd would keep a close eye on Bella. She didn't know if Bella was guilty, but she couldn't afford to take any chances. Not when their lives were at stake.

Clary left the kitchen, her mind spinning with questions. As she made her way down the hall, she nearly collided with Ethan.

"I'm glad I found you," he said, gently grabbing her arm. "Please, just listen to me."

Clary paused, looking up at him. The earnestness in his eyes made her want to believe him, to trust he was innocent.

"I know it seems bad, but you have to believe me, I would never hurt Brenna," said Ethan. "Whatever she thought was between us, I didn't reciprocate it. You have to trust me."

Clary hesitated. She wanted to believe him, but her instincts as an amateur detective were screaming not to let down her guard. "Okay," she finally said with caution, aware she couldn't fully trust him now. "I'll continue working with you to figure this out, but no more secrets, deal?"

Ethan nodded, relief flooding his expression. "Deal. Thank you, Clary."

As they continued searching the house together, Clary pushed down the doubts trying to resurface. She couldn't afford to blindly trust anyone, even Ethan. After all, he had motive and opportunity if he was telling the truth about Brenna's unwanted advances. And his hair had been wet moments after she saw Brenna lying in the soaking rain...

She glanced at him discreetly, noticing again how handsome he was. No, she had to stay objective. For now, she would work with him but keep up her guard. The bracelet found with the body was still the biggest question mark. Why would the real killer leave such an obvious clue pointing to her?

Obviously, they wanted her to seem like the perpetrator. She shivered. Ethan had seemed so quick to trust her again, despite that damning evidence. Was it an act? Had he known she couldn't be the murderer because *he* was?

She shook herself. Time would reveal the truth. For now, she had to remain vigilant and keep investigating. The killer was still at large, and she couldn't let her conflicted feelings cloud her judgment.

Clary sighed wistfully, imagining herself back in her cozy cottage with Mr. Darcy's soft fur under her fingers, and a warm cup of chamomile tea steaming on the table beside her. No confusing crushes or convoluted murder mysteries to untangle. Just the blank screen waiting patiently for her words. Rather than dread the prospect of writing, as she'd done far too often, she couldn't wait to immerse herself in the process again. Being near a murder must be the cure for writer's block.

If only she could transport herself back there right now, leaving this Gothic nightmare behind. But the image quickly faded as Ethan's voice pulled her back to the present.

"Clary? Did you hear that?"

She blinked, focusing on him. "Hear what?"

"Listen."

A second later, a loud scream shattered the silence.

Chapter Eleven

CLARY TENSED AS ANOTHER bloodcurdling scream pierced the air. She exchanged an alarmed look with Ethan before they both took off running down the hall.

They arrived breathless in the foyer to find Bella sprawled dramatically across the marble floor. Above her, one of the stone gargoyles that adorned the walls was now lying cracked on the floor, its tail shattered.

"It almost crushed me," cried Bella, throwing a hand across her forehead.

Clary rushed over to help her up, glancing suspiciously at the mostly intact gargoyle. "What happened?"

"I was just walking by, and it suddenly broke free and fell. If I hadn't jumped back in time..." Bella trailed off, dabbing at imaginary tears.

Clary helped Bella to her feet, noting her calm demeanor despite the theatrics.

"Let's take a closer look at this gargoyle," said Ethan, moving toward the rubble.

Clary nodded, following him over. As Ethan examined the mounting hooks, she scanned the debris. Her gaze snagged on a few shiny smudges along a broken edge. Leaning closer, she saw it was pink polish. And not just any pink—it was the exact bubblegum shade Bella was sporting on her fingers right now.

"What do we have here?"

Ethan turned, spotting the incriminating evidence. Understanding flashed in his eyes.

"Bella," he asked evenly, "Would you care to explain how your nail polish ended up on this gargoyle?"

Bella's face reddened, but she held her chin high. "I have no idea what you're talking about."

"I think you do," said Clary. "Just admit what really happened here."

"How dare you?" Bella shrieked. "I was nearly killed, and you imply... I'm leaving! won't stand here and be accused of fabricating my own murder."

"Attempted," said Ethan with a hint of humor that Clary admired, because the word had sprung to her lips too.

With a fierce glare, she flounced away, leaving only the scent of her floral perfume behind.

Clary met Ethan's gaze. "That went about as well as an artichoke tasting contest."

Ethan chuckled. "She's clearly hiding something. We'll have to keep pressing her."

Clary nodded, but uncertainty still plagued her. This whole situation made her feel like she was performing surgery with a chainsaw instead of a scalpel. And the nagging thought of that planted bracelet kept poking at her confidence.

She sighed. "Let's take another look around. Maybe we missed a clue earlier."

As they moved through the mansion's creepy halls, she tried to focus on the task at hand, but doubts kept sneaking in, eroding her usual plucky resolve. She could only hope that together, she and Ethan could find the killer before her name was carved onto a gravestone.

Clary and Ethan made their way to the library, hoping to find more clues. As they entered, they saw Martha and Timothy sitting near the fireplace, engrossed in hushed conversation. They looked up as Clary and Ethan approached. "Did you find anything new?" asked Martha.

Clary quickly filled them in on the suspicious gargoyle incident with Bella.

"She's clearly staging attacks to divert suspicion," said Ethan.

Martha shook her head. "Maybe it's just for attention and to be acknowledged as important. That poor girl. Brenna really did a number on her."

Clary nodded sympathetically. "Still, her actions are pretty incriminating. It makes me wonder..."

She trailed off, thinking back to the chandelier incident. At the time, she'd dismissed Bella's involvement. But now...

"You think she had something to do with the chandelier too?" asked Timothy, clearly following her train of thought.

"It's possible," said Ethan. "Can anyone confirm where Bella was when it happened, or when what happened to Brenna...happened?"

The others exchanged uncertain looks and shook their heads.

"I think she was alone when the chandelier fell..." Timothy frowned. "I saw her in the hallway last night, but I just remembered she told you she'd been in her room all evening."

Clary's eyes widened. "That's a major hole in her story."

If Bella had lied about her whereabouts, it made her look even more suspicious. Clary felt they were finally making headway in the investigation but doubt still lingered. She couldn't shake the thought Bella might just be a pawn in the real killer's twisted game. Framing others to divert attention from themselves, like they'd tried to do to her by planting her bracelet. Being a drama queen didn't make one a murderer. But maybe it helped make one a murderer?

"I think we should search her room and also check for physical evidence linking her to the attacks," said Clary.

"That's such an invasion..." Martha trailed off with a sigh and nodded. "Yes, I suppose we must."

Once she agreed, the others quickly fell in line, and they walked quietly upstairs moments later.

As they crept toward Bella's room, Clary turned to Timothy. "What's your take on Bella? Have you noticed anything odd about her behavior in the past?"

Timothy hesitated, pushing his glasses up his nose. "There was this one time at a writer's conference when she really laid it on thick. She kept name-dropping famous authors she'd supposedly met with and boasted about sales numbers I knew were exaggerated."

Ethan cleared his throat. "I saw her at a convention once. She was trying really hard to impress this well-known fantasy author. I got the sense she likes to stretch the truth if it gets her attention."

Clary nodded thoughtfully. "Interesting. What about you, Martha? Have you seen anything questionable in how Bella conducts herself?"

Martha pursed her lips. "I've observed her cozying up to certain people—editors, bloggers, and influential authors. She's strategic about who she befriends and how." She lowered her voice, looking embarrassed by association. "At one industry party, she feigned getting tipsy and spilled a sob story to the host. You all know David Tyers." How could they not? "He ended up introducing her to all the top agents there." She raised her eyebrows meaningfully at Clary. "Bella knows how to work people to get ahead. I wouldn't put staging attacks past her."

Clary absorbed this, fitting it with her own observations of Bella's thirst for fame and penchant for drama. The image of a calculating, spotlight-craving persona was sharpening.

If Bella was so willing to manipulate situations to her benefit, manufacturing attacks to look innocent made perfect sense. Clary felt they must be on the right track. Hopefully the room search would provide the final proof they needed.

"All right, let's keep moving, but quietly—we don't want Bella to know we're onto her." Clary motioned them forward, hoping the end of this mystery was finally in sight.

As they stealthily approached Bella's room, Clary shivered with anticipation and apprehension. The hallway was shrouded in darkness, save for the dim glow of a distant lamp. Each creaking floorboard beneath their feet echoed like a thunderclap in the quiet of the night.

Chapter Twelve

CLARY'S MIND RACED, connecting the dots between Bella's manipulative tactics and the unsettling events that had unfolded. If Bella was willing to bend the truth and use others to further her career, it was clear why she'd want Brenna out of the way. She might have felt Brenna was holding her back and picking on her instead of recognizing that she needed to develop her skills further.

But why kill Adrian? That was the lingering question. It didn't seem like she had killed him out of necessity, as if he had discovered her murdering Brenna. No, his death had been personal, an act of vengeance carried out in his own room while he slept.

Their footsteps barely made a sound as they approached Bella's door. Clary's hand trembled slightly as she turned the doorknob, hoping to find some piece of evidence that would shed light on the truth they sought.

Inside Bella's room, the air felt heavy with anticipation. Clary's eyes scanned the surroundings, searching for any clue that would reveal Bella's true intentions. Her gaze landed on a desk, upon which lay a stack of letters.

With bated breath, Clary picked up one of the letters and began to read. The words spilled forth like a confession, a testimony of the secret affair between Bella and Adrian. The letters started as passionate love notes, recounting stolen moments and whispered promises, but as Clary continued to read, the tone shifted.

Adrian's words became solemn, his guilt apparent. He expressed his desire to end the affair, to devote himself to his marriage and repair the damage caused by their illicit relationship. He pleaded with Bella to understand and to let go, urging her to find happiness outside of their forbidden connection.

The realization hit Clary like a tidal wave. Bella's motive for wanting Adrian gone became clear. She was consumed by jealousy and resentment, unable to bear the thought of him leaving her behind and going back to his wife. Hadn't she spoken disparagingly of Adrian's wife when they came to tell him about Brenna's death and found him also dead? Wifey something...? The letters were a window into her desperation and determination to hold onto something that was slipping away.

Clary's looked closer at the ink on the letters, sure they were written by an old-fashioned fountain pen by the tilt of the words and the drips of ink—a pen like the one used to stab Adrian through the heart. It was a chilling realization, the pieces of the puzzle falling into place. Bella's love had turned to hatred, her obsession with Adrian leading her down a dark path. Had Brenna seen her kill Adrian and run into the night? If so, why hadn't she called for help?

Clary carefully placed the letters back on the desk, her hands trembling with a mix of apprehension and resolve. They had found the evidence they needed, the undeniable connection between Bella, the affair, and Adrian's murder. It was time to confront her, to bring the truth to light and ensure justice was served.

Taking a deep breath, Clary turned to her companions, determination shining in her eyes. "We have what we need," she said, her voice steady. "It's time to confront Bella and put an end to this."

As Clary and her companions turned, their gazes met with Bella standing in the doorway of her room. A mix of surprise and indignation flashed across her face as she took in their presence.

FATAL CORRECTIONS

"What do you think you're doing in my room?" Bella exclaimed, her voice laced with outrage. "This is a violation of my privacy."

Clary's expression remained resolute as she stepped forward, closing the distance between them. "We have reason to believe that you're involved in the events that have unfolded."

Bella scoffed, crossing her arms defensively. "Involved? That's absurd. You have no evidence to support such accusations."

Clary held Bella's gaze. "Oh, but we do. We've gathered information, accounts from others, and found damning evidence that points directly to you."

Bella's eyes widened, a flicker of fear and realization momentarily crossing her features. "You're bluffing." She tossed her blonde hair, her voice quivering with defiance and apprehension.

Clary extended the stack of Adrian's letters. With deliberate movements, she handed them to Bella. "Read these," she said, her tone cutting through the tension. "They're letters written by Adrian to you, detailing your affair and his intention to end it. Of course, you don't need to read them, do you? And they're written in ink with a fountain pen, aren't they?"

She refused to take the letters. "He was so pretentious with his old fountain pens and bottles of ink. He even typed on an antique typewriter and never joined social media." She curled her lip. "That doesn't make me a murderer."

Timothy stepped forward, his voice calm yet firm. "We've also witnessed your manipulative tactics—your attempts to use others, stretch the truth, and gain an advantage in your career."

Martha nodded in agreement. "You cozy up to influential people, feign emotions, and strategically work your way into advantageous situations," she said, her voice tinged with disappointment. "All for the sake of your own ambition."

Bella's face paled as the weight of their words sinking in. She seemed momentarily overwhelmed, her emotions teetering on the edge. Then

73

her expression became defiant again. "That doesn't make me a murderer. It just gives me a leg up on pathetic losers like all of you."

"Who did you kill first?" asked Ethan.

Bella stiffened but didn't answer.

"I think it must have been Adrian, and Brenna caught her in the act. Bella decided what was one more?" said Clary.

Bella sneered, and then, in a surge of impulsive reaction, she shoved Clary away and bolted out of the room, her footsteps echoing down the hallway.

Clary stumbled back from the force of Bella's shove, her balance momentarily disrupted. As she struggled to regain her footing, her voice rang out, laced with determination and urgency. "After her! Go!" Clary called out to her companions, her words cutting through the chaotic atmosphere. "I'll catch up!"

They dashed after Bella, their footsteps echoing through the corridors as they pursued her into the surrounding area, determined to capture her and uncover the truth that lay hidden within her actions.

Clary fought to regain her balance, her shoes sliding on the polished floor. She flailed her arms, desperately trying to steady herself before finally finding her footing. By the time she regained her balance, her companions had already rushed past her, their hurried footsteps echoing through the hallway.

Breathing heavily, Clary quickly composed herself. She couldn't waste any more time. With a renewed sense of urgency, she hurried down the staircase, her footsteps a frantic echo against the grand foyer.

As Clary reached the bottom of the stairs, she caught a glimpse of Bella's figure disappearing through the open front door. The storm outside raged on, rain pouring down in torrents, and the wind howling with unrestrained fury. Ignoring her drenched clothes and the gusts that threatened to push her back, Clary pushed forward, determined to catch up with Bella.

With each step she took, the distance between them seemed to stretch, but Clary's resolve burned brightly within her. She navigated the slick pathway, her shoes slipping on the wet ground. Her heart raced, fueled by adrenaline, as she pushed herself harder, closing the gap between them.

The rain plastered Clary's hair to her face, blurring her vision, but she pressed on, her determination fueling her. Every stride brought her closer to Bella, her goal fixed in her mind—to apprehend her and uncover the truth. She needed to know who killed Brenna to prove it wasn't her, since Bella had ensured her bracelet was linked to Brenna in death.

Her lungs burned with exertion, and her legs felt heavy, but Clary refused to give in. She gritted her teeth, her eyes locked on Bella's retreating form. With each step, she could feel the gap closing, resolve driving her forward.

The wind whipped at Clary's drenched clothes, threatening to pull her off-balance, but she fought against its force, her eyes fixed on the figure ahead, her focus adamant. The storm raged around her, mirroring the turmoil within her own mind.

Through sheer willpower, Clary surged forward. She strained to see through the rain-soaked dimness as the sun rapidly faded from the sky, her heart pounding with each passing moment.

As Clary's strides quickened, she closed the distance between them. The sound of her pounding footsteps merged with the drumming rain, creating a symphony of pursuit in the midst of the storm. She could almost taste victory though her breath came in short gasps.

With every ounce of strength left within her, Clary pushed herself, desperate to catch up with Bella. The pursuit had become a race against time and the elements, and she was determined to cross the finish line.

Chapter Thirteen

FINALLY, CLARY CAUGHT up with Bella just as she reached a secluded spot outside. Panting heavily, she confronted her, her voice edged with a mix of determination and curiosity. "Bella," Clary called out, her voice slightly breathless. "Wait."

Bella turned, her face a mask of surprise mixed with a tinge of defiance. "What do you want?" she snapped, her voice dripping with hostility.

Clary took a step closer, her gaze unwavering. "I want to know how my bracelet ended up in your possession," she said, her voice firm. "And why you used it to frame me."

Bella's eyes flickered, her expression momentarily betraying a hint of guilt. She clenched her fists, her lips pressing into a tight line. The tension in her body spoke volumes, revealing a mix of jealousy and resentment.

"You think you're so perfect, Clary." Her voice was filled with bitterness. "Everyone adores you, while I'm constantly overlooked. I wanted to show them your flaws, to make them doubt you."

Clary furrowed her brows, trying to comprehend Bella's intense reaction. Their limited acquaintance made Bella's animosity all the more puzzling. She took a deep breath, her voice steady. "We barely know each other. Why would you go to such lengths to frame me?"

"Because you should suffer instead of me." Her expression twisted. "Like Brenna suffered. I watched Adrian struggling to breathe, and I knew it would be even more satisfying to end her."

"How did you do it?" She didn't really expect Bella to answer, so she was surprised when she spoke again.

"She was in the sunroom editing something by candlelight. Just as pretentious and ridiculous as Adrian, with his refusal to embrace modern technology. It was probably your next great masterpiece she was making bleed red with that wretched red pen of hers." Her expression contorted with fury and bitterness. "She knew. Somehow, she knew..."

"Knew what?"

"That I was there to kill her. She took one look at me and ran outside. She never called for help. Maybe the old witch panicked." She let out a cold laugh. "I scooped up the pen and followed her. I chased her down and stabbed her just like she deserved."

Clary shivered, and it wasn't just from the cold rain. "Okay." She pretended that didn't disturb her. "So why frame me?" she asked again. "We barely know each other."

Bella's face contorted with a mix of frustration and envy. "It's not fair," she said, her voice filled with resentment. "You have everything handed to you, and I'm left in your shadow. I wanted to make them see that you're not as perfect as they think."

"I understand that it may seem that way from the outside, but trust me, nothing was handed to me," Clary said, her voice filled with sincerity. "I've worked tirelessly for my success, just like anyone else, and I certainly haven't had it easy."

Bella's face contorted with a mix of frustration and envy, her resentment seeping through her words. "It's easy for you to say," she said, her voice tinged with bitterness. "You have talent, connections, and opportunities that I could only dream of. It's like you effortlessly sail through life while I'm left struggling."

Clary shook her head, her voice filled with empathy. "I've had my fair share of challenges and setbacks. For years, I worked alongside Brenna, enduring her harsh critiques and comparisons. It was far from an easy journey. Success came through perseverance, learning from my mistakes, and embracing the opportunities that came my way."

She paused, her gaze meeting Bella's with sincerity. "We all have our own unique journeys, and each one is filled with its own hurdles and triumphs. Rather than tearing each other down, let's find ways to support and uplift one another. We're both capable of achieving great things."

After a moment, Bella snorted. "You should write greeting cards instead of romances with that drivel coming out of your mouth."

Clary sighed, recognizing it was the worst sort of drivel, though she'd been trying to get through to the other woman. "Why don't we go back inside?"

"Why don't you...jump off a cliff?" As she said that, Bella lunged forward, striking Clary's shoulders with her hands.

Clary stumbled backward, looking over her shoulder and noticing she wasn't far from the rocky slope that ended in a deep drop to the beach below. She tried veering toward the wooden stairs carved into the cliff face instead, though they didn't look a lot safer. "Enough people have died—"

Bella laughed. "One more can't hurt...well, maybe it'll hurt *you*."

As the tension escalated, her heart sank at Bella's venomous words. The sincerity in her earlier plea for understanding seemed to have fallen on deaf ears. The disappointment mixed with a surge of anger, fueling a dangerous fire within her.

"You really think resorting to violence is the answer?" Clary's voice trembled with a mix of frustration and disbelief. "We're better than this. We can rise above our differences and find a way to move forward."

But Bella's laughter echoed in the air, mocking and cruel. The sound grated against Clary's nerves, intensifying her determination to protect herself and end this futile confrontation. As Bella lunged forward, striking Clary's shoulders with force, Clary stumbled backward, her body fighting to maintain balance.

As Bella lunged at her again, Clary stumbled backward another step, now dangerously close to the cliff's edge. Her foot hit a loose rock, and she pinwheeled her arms, trying to regain her balance.

Bella bore down on her, face contorted in rage. In that moment, the rickety wooden stairs caught Clary's gaze. If she could just make it there...

She dodged past her in a desperate bid for the stairs, but Bella grabbed her arm, yanking her back. They grappled perilously close to the cliff before she broke away and reached the stairs.

They swayed with her as she clung to the railing. Clary didn't want to move forward, but Bella didn't hesitate, clearly too focused on ending Clary to pay attention to the state of the staircase. She stepped on one and then another. With a sickening crack, the wooden step Bella stood on gave way.

She shrieked, arms flailing as she toppled backward. Clary lunged forward, trying to catch her hand, but their fingers slipped apart. She was still reaching even as the other woman continued hurtling toward the beach.

Bella's scream cut off abruptly as she slammed into the jagged rocks below. Clary staggered back, horrified. She peered over the cliff's edge at Bella's lifeless body, bile rising in her throat.

Footsteps pounded toward her. Ethan and the others had heard the commotion. Clary turned to them with tear-filled eyes.

"It was an accident," she choked out. "The stairs collapsed, and she fell."

The others exchanged grim, stunned looks. Despite everything, no one had wanted this outcome. Ethan moved swiftly to Clary's side, gently turning her away from the horrific sight. "It's over now," he said, enveloping her in his strong arms.

Clary collapsed against him, finally allowing the emotions to crash over her like a tidal wave. She clung to Ethan as sobs wracked her body, the trauma of the past few days pouring out of her. Ethan just held her close, providing a solid anchor amidst the storm.

After what felt like an eternity, Clary's tears slowed to a trickle. She lifted her head from Ethan's chest, suddenly conscious of their proximity. His steadfast compassion and warmth had gotten her through the worst of the shock.

"Thank you," she whispered, not yet ready to leave the safety of his embrace.

Ethan gave her a tender smile. "Of course. We've been in this together from the start." Their shared trauma had created an unbreakable bond that filled Clary with gratitude and the stirrings of something more.

In the distance, the faint drone of an approaching boat interrupted the moment. Help was on the way at last. As it drew near, Clary spotted the word "Police" printed on the side.

One of the officers called up to them as the boat slowed to a stop. "We got a call from a concerned family member..." He looked down at something in his hand before looking up again. "An Emily Lane...about a loss of contact. Are you folks okay?"

"Pretty far from actually," she said with a slightly hysterical giggle as Ethan took her hand.

As she and Ethan, with Timothy and Martha following behind, descended to meet the authorities, there were still questions to answer and trauma to unpack, but with Ethan's steady presence beside her, she had the strength to face whatever came next. The nightmare was over at last.

Epilogue

A FEW HOURS LATER, Clary stood on the shore watching the last traces of the island disappear over the horizon. It was hard to believe that just this morning, they had still been trapped in that nightmare.

Now, as the setting sun cast a warm glow across the beach, it almost felt like it had happened to different people, but the lingering trauma in her heart told Clary it had been all too real.

Beside her, Ethan slipped his hand into hers. "How are you holding up?"

Clary managed a small smile. "Better now that it's over. Still processing everything." She turned to face him. "I don't think I could have gotten through this without you by my side."

Ethan brushed a windblown brown curl from her face. "Ditto. We work well together." They gazed at each other, the air between them charged with emotion. "Come visit me in New York when you're ready," Ethan said softly. "I want to show you the city. Take you to all my favorite places."

Joy bubbled up in Clary's heart. "I'd love that." No matter what the future held, Ethan would be a part of it.

HOME SWEET HOME. AFTER the absolute carnival funhouse of horror that was amateur sleuthing and nearly getting murdered on that wretched island, Clary was thrilled to be back in her quaint and cluttered cottage in Michigan's UP. She sank into her trusty armchair with an "Oof," the well-worn leather enveloping her like a cozy hug from grandma—if grandma smelled like ancient books and cat hair.

Late afternoon sun filtered through the perpetually dusty windows, casting everything in a nostalgic sepia tone. At her feet, Mr. Darcy let out a meow that sounded suspiciously like "Feed me, human slave." Clary rolled her eyes affectionately.

"Yeah, yeah, Your Highness. Keep your fur on."

Her gaze drifted to the blank page on her laptop, the blinking cursor awaiting her next masterpiece, and inspiration struck like a lightning bolt. Only instead of lightning, it was more like a gentle tap on the shoulder from the elusive Muse.

She began typing furiously, crafting a thrilling tale of secrets, suspicion, and a murder most foul. Hey, she couldn't let that first-hand near-death experience go to waste. Maybe she'd even throw in a dashing love interest who was smart, courageous, and didn't completely suck. A girl could dream, and she didn't want to disappoint her readers by skimping on the romance.

As she wrote, thunder rumbled in the distance, a dramatic rumble of approval, as if nature itself joined in on the excitement. The world outside was a symphony harmonizing with Clary's creative flow. Words poured out of her like a waterfall cascading down a majestic cliff. Her fingers danced over the keys with a pleasing clicking sound, stitching together a tapestry of secrets, betrayal, and murder on the backdrop of an isolated island.

The road ahead still held bumps and potholes, but she was ready to pounce on opportunities like a cat on catnip. For now, she was exactly where she wanted to be—in her cozy haven, accompanied by a cranky cat and quirky characters. And with an impending visit to New York City and the promise of real romance for herself, not just her heroines, the future was looking as bright as Mr. Darcy's shiny fur.

At her feet, Mr. Darcy, her wise feline companion, stirred from his nap, his sage green eyes blinking at her as if to say, "I still require sustenance, servant." He punctuated it with a long meow, clearly showing her how much he suffered.

"All right, Mr. Darcy, I guess I could take a break to feed you." She stood up and stretched to scratch behind his ear before heading to the kitchen. While she fixed cat food, her mind was still writing, and she was looking forward to getting back to the grind for the first time in a long time. Her writer's block was broken. Between that and meeting Ethan, the writers' retreat hadn't been all bad.

About The Author

BORN AND RAISED IN the heartland of America, Delia's love for storytelling was nurtured by a childhood filled with books and the enchanting tales spun by her grandmother.

With a degree in English Literature from the University of Michigan, Delia honed her craft as a writer and developed a keen eye for the intricate details that make a story come alive. Her passion for mysteries was ignited by her love for Agatha Christie novels, and she has since dedicated her writing career to creating puzzling mysteries that keep readers guessing until the very end.

When she's not weaving her next tale of murder and intrigue, Delia enjoys gardening, baking, and exploring the beautiful trails of her home state. She lives with her husband and a mischievous cat named Sherlock, who serves as her writing companion and occasional source of inspiration. Her grandchildren love to visit, and Delia always drops everything, no matter whose murder awaits solving.

Receive information about new releases by subscribing to Dalia's newsletter[1].

Milton Keynes UK
Ingram Content Group UK Ltd.
UKHW020651070823
426447UK00015B/828